The Unpaid Internship

Joe Harrison

Published by Joe Harrison, 2021.

THE UNPAID INTERNSHIP

First edition. December 24, 2021.

ISBN: 979-8409015169

Written by Joe Harrison.

For my parents

Who I'm sure would agree raising me was a piece of
cake.

Chapter 1

"I'm sorry, but this isn't right."

Napoleon inspects the dress wrapped in a thin layer of plastic as he stands at the counter of the dry cleaners.

"Da, it's right," says the Russian woman sitting in a chair opposite him.

There's a mixture of perspiration and contempt on her face. The perspiration is likely a result of the lack of air-conditioning in the cramped, poorly lit, shopfront.

But as for the contempt, Napoleon isn't sure if it's her natural disposition from working in customer service, or if it's a special air that she's reserved just for him.

At least she's getting paid, he thinks.

"No, I get that this might be the dress that's connected to this number," he says, holding up the receipt he had been issued upon depositing the dress two days ago. "But the dress I'm supposed to pick up is a bright yellow."

When she says nothing, he elaborates further: "It has pockets, a black trim, and the name *Cindy* written on the label." He gestures to the dress on the counter. "This one's more of a flaxen color. It's got no pockets, at least, as far as I can tell. And there's no name on it."

In the pause that follows, the only sound of note is the whirring of a tiny desk fan rotating back and forth between himself and the Russian.

"You are special guy?" she asks.

His eyebrows launch upward. "Beg your pardon?"

"Food can't touch on plate?" She taps the side of her temple.

Holy shit.

"Nope, just detail-oriented," he says. "Could you please double-check that the other dress isn't back there?"

She gets up from her chair without another word and walks off into the litany of conveyor belts. Eventually, she returns with the right dress and he's able to walk out into the dusky Brooklyn evening.

The cold dark blue of the sky complements the yellow glow of the streetlights bouncing off the brownstone townhomes. A rat is dragging a used condom over to a sewer grate.

Napoleon's several blocks away from his apartment now and keen to get home. At this point, he would usually be getting ready to leave for his night job at Sal's Catering Service where he worked as a waiter.

The pay was dogshit, but it was good cardio, and he had figured that it would be a nice change of pace from the obvious mental demands of a journalism internship.

How naïve of me.

Tonight, however, is Napoleon's one night of the week off and there's a beer calling his name at the Next Best, his regular bar. Most nights, it's run by a bartender named Tommy. A decent fella who lets Napoleon and his friends drink for free, purely out of the kindness of his heart – and because he's sleeping with Napoleon's roommate Skylar.

Foot traffic is at a minimum and Napoleon's making good time. A text from Burger informs him that Burger and Skylar are already at the bar, and he should meet them there.

He decides to go home first so he can change out of his short-sleeve button-down and eat whatever's in the fridge for the sake of not drinking on an empty stomach.

As he's running through this itinerary in his head, he's paying little attention to where he's going and soon finds himself walking through a horde of bees.

Panic sets in almost immediately.

In the hope of putting some distance between himself and his attackers, he closes his eyes and flails his arms around like the world's worst boxer.

Thoroughly off-balance, he trips over a set of garbage cans and falls flat against the unforgiving concrete.

"Ow," he wheezes.

As he lies there in the entryway to a grimy-looking alley, his ears ringing and the wind knocked out of him, he wonders how expensive it'll be to go to the emergency room, given that he has no insurance.

It takes a minute for him to sit upright.

After he does, the first thing he checks is that the dress wasn't damaged in the fall. Deciding it passes inspection, he turns to his own well-being. His ribs feel bruised but not broken. His forearm is cut from where it hit the ground, but the ringing in his ears is subsiding.

Rising to his feet, he notices a set of legs protruding out from behind a dumpster farther down the alley. He quickly looks away, assuming it to be just another homeless man getting some much-needed shut-eye. Then a thought enters his mind that gives him pause:

Fancy shoes for a homeless man.

He looks back at the legs. And sure enough, whoever they belong to is sporting a pair of $3.000 loafers that appear unaccustomed to the streets of New York.

The trousers tell a similar story: recently ironed, none of the weathering common amongst the clothes of the city's homeless. They could've qualified as spotless if not for the blood.

"Blood," Napoleon says. "That's . . . you're bleeding. Help! Somebody get some help!"

He runs over to the dumpster to find a Caucasian man sitting upright against the brick wall of the alley. He's unconscious. Or dead. Definitely one of the two.

His face is also seriously bruised. And three bullet holes in his chest are contributing to an ever-widening pool of red around his body.

Not ideal.

"Hey," Napoleon whispers as he moves towards the man. "Hey, please don't be dead."

A part of Napoleon wants to try and wake the man up. But another, smarter part is telling him that if the man was dead, then putting a handprint on his bullet-riddled corpse would be unwise. In the end, a third option wins out.

"Nine-one-one what is your emergency?" the operator at the other end of the line asks.

"Yes? Hello? I've just found someone bleeding out in an alley. It looks like he's been shot, and I think he might be dead."

"All right, sir, please remain calm. Is the shooter still in the area?"

"No idea."

"As far as you can tell, is there anyone or anything in the area posing an immediate threat to your life?"

"Well, not that I'm aware of, I'm more concerned about this other guy to be honest."

"An ambulance is en route to your location. Have you identified a pulse?"

"No, that's when you put the two fingers up against the neck, right?"

"Yes, sir. You're going to want to place your index and middle finger just to the side of the windpipe. Or if you're unable to reach it, you could try and locate a pulse at the base of his wrist. But if he doesn't look to be breathing, I suggest the neck."

"You'd suggest?"

"I'd recommend the neck."

"Explain to me why you think that's better?!"

With a sudden intake of breath, the man jolts, and his eyes shoot open. His inhalation is so loud that it catches Napoleon off guard, causing him to drop the call.

"Wha—"

Before Napoleon can finish his thought, the man's pulled him forward by the fabric of the dress he's still holding in his free hand.

"Woah, easy." He struggles to regain his balance. "Try not to move. Help is on the way, but you've lost some blood."

Desperate pants escape the man's lungs in between gargled coughs. Blood trickles out of his mouth as his head rolls from side to side, presumably so he can find his bearings. It does a whole lot of nothing to instill Napoleon with confidence about the man's chances of survival.

"Someone shot you," Napoleon says. "But I'm guessing you knew that already. Come to think of it, you wouldn't happen to know if the shooter's still around by chance, would you?"

A look of surprise falls over the man's face as though he's just now realizing someone else is there with him.

"Sorry," Napoleon says, "I don't know if I should be trying to keep you talking or not. Every movie I've seen where the guy's bleeding out, his buddy's trying to keep him awake until backup arrives and that's pretty much the extent of my understanding of these situations."

The man lets out a muffled murmur that only vaguely passes for a word.

"What was that?" Napoleon asks more alert now. "What are you trying to say?"

He's pulled forward again as the man musters up what's left of his strength to say something, presumably, of great importance or relevance to his current situation.

Then again, Napoleon thinks. *These could be his dying words.*

Napoleon isn't sure which option he likes less. But despite his feelings, he cups his ear and leans forward to make sure he doesn't miss a word. As soon as he does, the man shouts:

"COCKSUCKER!"

"Ah! The fuck?"

The man coughs up more blood as an ambulance's siren pulls Napoleon's focus upward. He strains his hearing as he frantically glances back and forth to either end of the alley, assuming the sound is the same ambulance he called for.

Intuition tells him to go right. Towards the bus stop. And he takes off at full tilt. He narrowly manages to avoid an oncoming car. Only to immediately find himself staring down the flashing lights of an ambulance.

The driver slams on the horn. And Napoleon interprets this to mean he should jump up and down while frantically pointing at the alley. Per his instructions, the ambulance cuts a hard left and quickly decelerates to a stop. At which point, two EMTs emerge and rush over to help the dying man.

"You made the 911 call?" one of them asks Napoleon as he approaches.

"Yeah," he says, picking up the dress. There's a hole in the plastic from where the man grabbed it and several bloody handprints have stained the fabric.

Terrific.

"The police are going to want to get a statement from you about what happened. You're welcome to ride with us and give it to them at the hospital, or you can just wait around until the responding officer gets here."

"Oh, uh, okay."

"But this guy's in critical condition, so you need to decide like yesterday."

"Right . . . Shit, I guess, I'll come with you guys."

"Then get in."

***

The hitman sets the metal briefcase down on the passenger seat as he climbs in behind the wheel of the hatchback. The knife he had also taken from the target is wrapped in cling film to prevent the blood splatter on it from spreading. The car will be cleaned before it's returned to the dealership regardless of these precautions.

The knife looks custom. Its design is similar to a military-issued Ka-Bar, but its weight and proportions suggest it isn't standard issue. There's also a tube on either side running down the length of the blade to its handle.

More examination will follow. Right now, he must deal with the wound on his shoulder. The sneaky son of a bitch had nicked him in the scuffle. And the blood wasn't clotting.

He slides the silenced Colt Model 1911 under his seat so it's easily within reach before retrieving a key from his coat. At which point, he leans over, unlocks the glove box, and pulls out a first aid kit.

The wound's going to need stitches, but he'll have to deal with it back at the motel. So long as the blood stops dripping down his arm, for the time being, he can focus on more pressing matters.

For example, he'd been given bad intel.

A superficial search of the target's person proved ineffective in locating the item he'd been instructed to recover. So he had taken the briefcase with him as he'd left. With any luck, it would have what he was looking for inside. Both his pay and professional reputation depended on it.

With the wound tended to, priority number one becomes opening the briefcase. He frowns as he realizes upon closer examination that he doesn't have the tools to open it.

The sounds of laughter emanating from outside the car prompt him to look up and see a group of people walking across the street.

If he's on a job and has a choice between street parking and a lot, he always chooses the street; lots have cameras.

Still, that didn't mean it was smart to hang around too long afterward. Especially when one is openly bleeding.

He sets the briefcase back down on the seat and turns the key in the ignition. The engine springs to life without so much as a rumble.

God, I love electric motors.

Chapter 2

"You are kidding me, right?"

Napoleon can't quite believe what he's hearing. The unhealthy-looking woman checking a clipboard on the other side of the reception desk doesn't so much as a glance in his direction. "Afraid not."

"Three months?" he asks, still unsure that he's heard correctly. "You're honestly telling me that if I wanted to use your laundry service for *one* item of clothing, I would, in fact, be waiting three months to get it back?"

"That's correct."

"Are you outsourcing the department to a company in Western Australia? How could it possibly take three months?"

"Dude, I'm just an assistant."

This is false. She's a nurse, not an assistant. She was also more than capable of helping Napoleon out. The hospital had cleaning equipment. If she wanted to, she could have his dress back to him in several hours. At most.

The truth is that her entire job consisted of caring for others. And while she enjoyed her work for the most part, occasionally, it did get to be a bit too much. The disease, the despair, the demands of both patients and families alike.

So to keep herself sane, now and then, she'd inconvenience someone. Never on anything life or death, of course. And never other staff; shitting where she ate held absolutely no appeal to her whatsoever.

However, from time to time, she'd been known to drop hints about perfectly functioning elevators being out of order and the cafeteria being closed several hours before it was. Just fun, quirky things.

"What if I said it was for my boss?" he asks. "Who needs it for tomorrow night. And who already doesn't like me, so showing up with her favorite article of clothing completely covered in blood will pretty much guarantee that I get fired?"

"I'd tell you to start applying for other jobs cuz it takes three months."

Napoleon can feel his eye twitching. The main reason he'd accepted a ride to the hospital is that he desperately needed to get the dress cleaned. Again.

"Can you at least help me out with a shirt?" he asks.

She looks up from her clipboard. The ambulance ride had been eventful, to say the least. The dying man's blood-filled coughing had grown worse, and Napoleon's shirt had borne the brunt of the spray.

"I can offer you wet wipes," she says, picking up a packet from off the reception desk and holding them out to him.

He stares blankly at her. Then at the wet wipes. Then back at her again.

"Dab," she says. "Don't rub."

He deflates, accepts the wipes. And shuffles over to a row of chairs along the outer wall of patient rooms. Setting the dress down on one of the chairs, he collapses into its neighbor and exhales.

The last few hours were a blur. A chaotic, stressful, blur. It's proving difficult to process.

All Napoleon had wanted was a beer and a few laughs to celebrate the one night off for the next few weeks. He shakes his head to try and eradicate all thoughts of the poor man clinging to life in the operating room down the hall. The last thing he wanted right now was perspective.

He briefly dabs at the blood on his shirt before realizing it's doing about as much good as a lint roller on a sheep.

Anxious, he decides to look up the laundromat's hours on his phone instead. It closes at ten. A glance at his watch tells him it's nearly nine. He can probably make it, but he would have to take a cab. Which he isn't sure he can afford, and he still hadn't spoken to—

"You're the witness?"

He looks up to see two Caucasian suits standing over him. One's a large, balding fucker in his fifties. There's both animosity and mutton chops on his chinless face.

The other's maybe twenty years younger than his buddy, with an athletic build, medium brown hair, and a stoic demeanor.

"Yeah. I mean yes, sirs."

"Detective Cayden Freeman," the athletic man says in a thick southern accent as he extends his hand out toward Napoleon. "This is my partner, Detective Douglas Hill."

"Napoleon Davis."

Having shaken Cayden's hand, Napoleon opts to extend the same courtesy to his partner, only to awkwardly withdraw a few seconds later when he realizes Douglas Hill has no intention of returning the gesture.

"We understand you were the one who discovered the body," Cayden says.

"Uh, yeah, I tripped over some garbage cans."

He goes on to give a brief overview of the events that followed. Detective Hill is quiet for the most part, offering little more than a contemptuous chuckle at several instances throughout his statement. The most notable time being when Napoleon recounts having noticed the man's shoes.

"Did he say anything to you?" Cayden asks. "Give you any indication as to what happened?"

"Not really. I asked. I thought I should try to keep him talking so he wouldn't shut his eyes, but he was in a bad way."

"Is," Douglas says.

"I'm sorry?"

"*Is* in a bad way. He's not dead yet."

"Right . . . Is in a bad way."

Cayden coughs. "And where were you coming from when you found him?"

"I was. Uh. Picking up a dry-cleaning order on 71st and 3rd."

Both men look puzzled as he gestures to the dress.

"It belongs to my boss."

"Anyone able to corroborate your story?" Cayden asks.

"Yeah, a Russian woman was working at the laundromat when I went in. I don't remember her name, but she was middle-aged and had shoulder-length brown hair."

"You see who shot him?" Douglas asks. Unlike Cayden, he isn't bothering to take any notes.

"No," Napoleon says, far more sternly than anticipated. "Sorry, but by the time I found him, whoever shot him was long gone."

He isn't certain, but Napoleon thinks he can make out Douglas muttering something about "convenience" under his breath.

"And the murder weapon?" Cayden asks, jotting down a note. "Was there any sign of that when you arrived?"

Napoleon shakes his head. "No, that doesn't mean it's not there though. I didn't do a lot of rooting around as you can imagine. You might want to search the area."

"Might we?" Cayden smiles.

"You a detective now?"

"No, I didn't mean —"

"Think you can tell us how to do our jobs?" Douglas asks.

"I'm just trying to help," Napoleon says softly.

"You know that we could pull you in for running from a crime scene?"

Napoleon gulps involuntarily, his mouth suddenly very dry. If that was true, why did the EMT tell him he could tag along? And why had nobody else said anything about it to him after he'd arrived?

His moment of contemplation gets cut short as the tense silence lingering in the air is then disrupted by a set of fast-approaching footsteps. Napoleon barely has time to steady himself as the next second, a fair-skinned blonde pushes through both detectives, lunges forward, and wraps her arms around his neck.

"Thank you!" she says in between pecks on his bewildered cheeks. "Thank you!" Kiss. "Thank you!" Kiss. "Thank you!"

"You're welcome," he says, more calmly than he feels. "What is it you're thanking me for exactly?"

"Saving." Kiss. "My husband's." Kiss. "Life."

She pulls away and cups his cheeks in her hands. Even with her swollen, tear-filled eyes, Napoleon can't help but acknowledge the divine quality of her beauty. Great tits, too.

Damn you, testosterone.

"The nurse said that if you hadn't called for help when you did. Milo would have . . ." She trails off, her face twisting as though even indulging the idea would be too painful.

"If there's anything you need." She hugs him again. "Ever. Anything at all."

A throat clearing prompts Napoleon to look back at Cayden, whose discomfort at the overt display of emotion has forced him to find something interesting on the far wall.

"Call us if you think of anything else," he says, holding out a business card toward Napoleon.

Napoleon takes it. And Cayden turns to go, releasing another hearty chest cough as he leaves. Douglas, on the other hand, stays put, his face riddled with disgust.

"You can't imagine what it's like getting a phone call saying . . ." The woman trails off. Like Napoleon, she's also now noticed Douglas. "Can I help you with something?" she asks.

Douglas grunts before waddling off after his partner without another word.

"Ma'am," the physician's assistant says, calling out to the woman from the reception desk, "I can take you to the observation deck now if you're ready."

"Oh, yes please!" She spins back to look at Napoleon. "I have to go now but . . . Thank you again. Truly." As she hurries off after the physician's assistant, she calls back to him, "You're my hero!"

Words failing him, he gives her a wave that borders on pathetic. Luckily, she doesn't see it. When she's gone, his focus returns to the dress.

He checks his watch; it's nine twenty. If he hauls ass, he might still be able to salvage one thing out of the wet soggy band-aid in the urine-riddled swimming pool that was his evening.

"Please let there be a cab out front."

***

The hitman parks behind a warehouse he had found on a public index of foreclosed properties. It's deserted, decrepit, and right next to the Hudson—an ideal location for what the night demands.

Exiting the hatchback, briefcase in hand, he walks over to the edge of the loading bay and sets it down so that it's waist level with himself. Having checked the gauze on his shoulder, he beelines for the shore beneath the pier, forgoing the need for a flashlight.

After half an hour of hopping across boulders and a handful of near stumbles, he finds a rock that meets his criteria. He had brought everything he might have needed for this job except a rotary cutter and now, in hindsight, it looked as though it should've been higher up on his list.

Yet there's an air of optimism to him as he hops back over to the warehouse. If his hunch is correct, he could finish the job tonight and be on the first plane out tomorrow morning.

Bracing the briefcase with his injured arm, he pulls his other arm back and slams the rock down on the lock with as much strength as he can gather. BLAM! It doesn't break.

It does, however, echo out across the warehouse thanks to the wide-open garage door off the loading bay. He draws air in through his teeth; it was sloppy not to have anticipated the echo.

He would have to open it on the second attempt now. The area's deserted for the time being, but loud noises had a habit of attracting loud creatures.

Having repositioned the briefcase so it's out of the way of the door, he adjusts the rock in his hand to improve his grip and takes several practice swings.

With his confidence renewed, he exhales before bringing the rock down against the lock. This results in a slightly more subdued echo reverberating out across the warehouse.

We'll call that a win.

At the same time, an anti-climactic clicking sound catches his attention. A glance down at the briefcase reveals the lock has given way under the rock's pressure and snapped; it's open.

What follows is a thorough inspection of its contents. Clothes, toiletries, a passport—it isn't there. The flash drive.

He empties the briefcase onto the loading dock as he begins to search it for hidden compartments. He checks for false bottoms, camouflaged linings, concealed switches.

Everything is triple-checked.

Upon realizing that this was to remain the world's shittiest treasure chest, he slams the briefcase's lid down in frustration.

"Hey!"

He hits the deck. Seconds later, a flashlight shines right over where he'd been standing. Staying prone, he swiftly crawls over to a rusty oil barrel and only just manages to get behind it before a security guard comes into view.

"I know you're out there!"

His remark's too vague to merit consideration as a real threat. Granted, both the suitcase and car were in plain view. But as far as the hitman can tell, he hasn't yet been made.

"Backup's on the way!"

Not likely.

It isn't until the guard kneels to inspect the suitcase that he decides to act. The gun isn't an option. Police would connect ballistics reports between kill zones.

Using the guard's fixation on the briefcase as a diversion, he makes his move. As he inches closer and his chances of success grow, his mind starts to relax.

Rock, paper, scissors, shoot. Rock, paper, scissors, shoot. Rock, paper, scissors—

BLAM!

Huh . . . rock wins.

He begins the process of removing any trace of himself from the pier. The dead guard is positioned to look as if he has been crushed by falling debris while the briefcase is repacked with the target's belongings and weighted down with several rocks.

Then it's dropped in the river at the edge of the pier.

To his surprise, a wave of nausea overwhelms him as he looks down at the current. It's so bad that he's forced to hold himself upright against a guardrail. He chuckles.

Guard.

There's the scent of rain in the air. Ambling back down the pier a short while later, he wonders if this might be his one last job. For a while anyway.

Chapter 3

"No."

"Yes."

"No."

"Yes!" Burger drops his fist onto the table. It takes very little force from his 220-pound frame to rattle the sizeable number of empty beer glasses on the wooden surface. He manages to catch one rolling toward the edge before the table lamp turns off. With a flick of its shade, the piercing-riddled face of his roommate, Skylar, is reilluminated across from him.

"How can you possibly think that's fair?" she asks, her tan arms folded across her chest.

"Because . . ." Burger pauses as their bartender approaches with another two lagers.

"Thanks, Tommy," Skylar says with a polite smile.

Tommy, the bartender, offers her a shy one in return before picking up the empties and continuing about his business.

"Right now, the water bill gets split three ways," Burger says. "It's the next biggest one behind the rent, and it's entirely because of you."

She lets out an appalled scoff.

"You take two baths a day," he adds. "A day! I shower once every three days."

"I'm well aware."

He ignores her comment. "How many jugs of water does it take to shower? How many does it take to fill a bath?"

"You wanna talk water usage?" She leans forward. "Let's do it. Do you know how often we have to mop the floors because of your muddy boots? You're incapable of using the same cup twice a day. Or any dish, come to think of it. Not that you ever wash them yourself, you just leave it for Napoleon and me to find whenever we get home."

"Find?" Burger looks puzzled. "What are you talking about *find*? I always put them in the dishwasher when I'm finished."

She touches her fingertips together to keep calm. "For the last time, that thing is not a dishwasher. It's a broken mini-fridge with a weird door. You have to wash the dishes by hand. I don't know why we keep having this conversation!"

Burger's about to offer a rebuttal when something catches his attention out of the corner of his eye. Noticing the change, Skylar follows his gaze over to the open front door of the Next Best. Both the murmurs of conversation around them and the band playing on stage have come to an abrupt halt.

Standing at the entrance is Napoleon, out-of-breath, drenched from the rain and wearing a disheveled shirt and tie that are splattered with a concerning color of red. He does his best to avoid the room's unblinking faces as he ambles over to the bar. As he nears, Tommy slides a lager his way, and Napoleon downs it enthusiastically.

"Much obliged," he says in a hushed whisper as he sets the empty glass against the counter. Tommy responds with a polite nod and a refill.

Both patrons and staff watch as Napoleon then carries his newly filled glass over to his friends' table. Puzzled looks pass between them as he sits down and takes another swig.

For a moment, nobody speaks.

"Band's good tonight," Napoleon says at last.

"Mm-hmm."

"Yep."

"You two had a good day?"

"Pretty good."

"Someone told me a funny joke today," Burger says, stroking his blonde beard. "Wanna hear it?"

"Please," Napoleon says.

"Okay. So," he picks up his beer. "A guy covered in blood walks into a bar—"

"Napoleon," Skylar interjects, "what the hell happened to you?!"

"It's been a rather eventful evening, friends."

For the second time that night, he explains how he stumbled upon the dying man. How he'd been questioned at the hospital. How he'd met his wife—the dying man's—and everything that had followed, all the way up to taking a taxi back across town to get to the dry cleaners before it shut.

"The lady working there was not happy about me walking in five minutes before they closed either. She said it would cost me double to have it ready in time for tomorrow night."

"You didn't try and find one closer to the hospital?" Skylar asks.

"I was pressed for time."

"The wife hot?"

Both Skylar and Napoleon turn toward Burger.

"What?" Napoleon asks.

"The guy's wife? Smokeshow? Yes, or no?"

"Yes, Burger. She was very good-looking."

Burger grins. "Nice."

"Anyways, I was hoping one of you might be able to lend me some money, just for a little while. The cab fee put me in an overdraft, and I don't get my paycheck from the catering company for another week."

His friends glance at each other.

"Napoleon," Skylar says, running fingers through her brown hair, "I'm sure I speak for both Burger and me when I say we sympathize with your situation, and we want to help you."

"But, buddy," Burger adds, "we're not exactly flushed for cash."

"Yeah, I mean, I've had ramen for dinner every night this week."

"And I'm still trying to pay off the money I owe my . . ." Burger trails off. "You know what? Never mind."

"Why don't you ask Cindy to reimburse you?" Skylar asks. "Surely, she doesn't expect you to pay for her dry cleaning. Is that even legal if you're an unpaid intern?"

"Trust me, she doesn't care," Napoleon says. "Besides, I'm not sure I want to rock the boat with her right now. I have a feeling she's finally about to give me my first writing assignment."

"You could always ask your parents for money," Burger suggests.

They all laugh.

"Or," he adds, having a sudden epiphany. "What you could do is ask the wife for money."

Skylar's brow furrows. "Come again?"

"What? She said if he ever needs anything, she'd be willing to help." He turns back to Napoleon. "Why not ask for a loan?"

"Because she's grieving, you ass!"

"No, she's celebrating. If Napo hadn't stopped to help, *then* she'd be grieving. And it's not like he's keeping the money. He's just trying to stay out of the red until he gets paid."

"It cheapens what you did though," Skylar says, addressing Napoleon. "Putting a dollar amount on saving a life like that is ugly."

"So's being poor." Burger chugs the rest of his beer and belches.

Napoleon glances back and forth between his friends. "I need to sleep on this." He finishes his drink. "Either of you want another?"

"I'll get them," Skylar offers. "I have to use the lady's room anyway."

This is partly true. She'd clocked that Tommy was only dealing with a handful of soaks and, for the moment, they were all nursing semi-full beers. Which meant he was just standing there, cleaning a glass with a towel.

She slows her pace as she passes by, making sure to catch his eye before disappearing down the corridor.

Reaching a lull in conversation, Napoleon shifts his focus back to the band. The smooth, jazz ensemble invites him to lean his head back against the wall and shut his eyes. With any luck, the melodies would simply carry away the stress of his day.

"Napoleon?"

"Yes, Burger?"

"That thing in the kitchen?"

"It's a mini-fridge, Burger."

***

The hitman uses his reflection in the bathroom mirror of his motel room to finish stitching up his shoulder wound. He had numbed the area, but, somewhat surprisingly, the pain was persisting.

With a final cut of the stitch thread, his wound is sealed, and he lets himself relax, only for nausea to return. He leans forward on the counter and lets out a stinky burp. The sweat dripping from his forehead prompts him to turn on the faucet and splash cold water on his face.

"What the hell," he groans.

This is troubling. There had been no deviations from his pattern of preparation in the lead-up to the job. He'd adhered to the workouts, diet, and sleep schedule necessary to minimize complications of this nature with a religious obsession.

Suddenly, a blanket of dizziness falls over him and the room begins to spin. At the same time, he hears the phone ringing in the bedroom. If he believed in fate, he would have thought she was being a dick.

He stumbles against the door frame, dresser, and desk before eventually reaching it, grateful not to have reopened the wound on his shoulder in the process.

"Hi, honey, how's college?" he asks into his cellphone.

"Nothing but sunshine and frisbees," comes a modulated voice through the receiver. "Our contract mandated you confirm by text an hour ago."

"There's been a complication."

"You think? He's alive! They've got him on an operating table right now!"

"He'll be dead soon."

"How can you be certain?"

"Professional competency." He stifles another burp.

Truth be told, this surprises him. Milo Eadwulf, the target, had taken three bullets right in the ten-ring. He had intended to shoot him in the head for good measure but had been spooked by what sounded like metal falling from a considerable height.

"He didn't have it," the hitman says, deciding to switch topics.

"What?" the voice asks. "You're sure?"

"I'm sure."

". . . Coordinates are N 40°46′30.9″, W 73°58′22.7″. Noon tomorrow. Don't be late."

He hangs up the phone and runs for the toilet, barely making it in time to avoid vomiting all over the floor. After several gut-wrenchingly awful minutes, he sits back on the cold tiles.

This isn't food poisoning, jet lag, or sleep deprivation as he initially suspected. The signs are evident now, and for the second time that night, he's kicking himself at his sloppiness.

Pushing off the wall, he hoists himself upright and heads back into the bedroom. The bag he's using as his portable office for this contract is on the chair in front of a large panel window currently hidden by a thick layer of curtains.

Inside, among killing-related other items, is the blade he'd stolen from Milo Eadwulf. He hasn't forgotten about its weight, or the odd tube lines running outwards from its handle. Studying it now, he can also see screws installed near its pommel and handguard.

This strikes him as strange; a two-sided hilt is uncommon for this type of knife, especially since it appears custom-made. Any engineer worth his 3D printer knows that a single-hilted blade is a far superior option when it comes to structural integrity.

Still dizzy, he reaches back into his backpack and searches about until he finds his multiheaded screwdriver. His vision blurs, and it takes longer than it should to unscrew the hilt.

Inside the handle, is a temperature-controlled hydraulic pump rigged to a release valve. From what he can gather, it's been designed to release a chemical into the bloodstream of whichever poor schmuck happens to be cut by its edge.

His instincts kick in at this revelation; he needs to move fast. He isn't sure how long the poison would take to kill him, but he has no intention of finding out.

Chapter 4

The next morning, Napoleon steps out of the elevator onto the main floor of the Epoch Tribune with two coffee carriers and a hangover. Per his routine, he'd picked them up from the break room several floors down for the various staff members in the office. Everyone's order was committed to memory his first day.

He sets the drinks down on the desks of their intended recipients as he navigates through the sea of cubicles until one remains.

Cindy Li's talent for breaking world-class stories had earned her numerous promotions over the years, in addition to an office overlooking the Manhattan skyline.

Her office door is presently shut, which means he still has time to gather himself before their daily meeting. They left the bar late last night, and Napoleon isn't a morning person at the best of times. This is especially unfortunate because today is important.

Six months ago, he dropped out of college for financial reasons, knowing it would hinder his career in journalism.

Fortunately, he managed to land an unpaid internship at a halfway decent rag that had promised him a full-time gig if he agreed to a "grace period" so they could evaluate his journalistic merits.

As a result, he spent the last couple of months as a glorified errand boy minus the glory, with little more than a verbal assurance that his first assignment was just around the corner.

Most days, he felt like a rabbit with a stick strapped to its back and a carrot dangling off the other end in front of his face.

But now, at long last, it looked like all that was coming to an end. Over the last few days, the hints had become more frequent.

Not from Cindy directly, of course.

Despite being his immediate supervisor, she didn't seem to pay attention to him at all, so long as he did what he was told.

The recent watercooler chat, however, was proving enlightening. Allegedly, she met with the managing editor several days ago and Napoleon's name had come up.

As far as he is concerned, it can't come fast enough. He is sick of spending long hours on mundane tasks with no pay, and no relevant experience. And he is definitely over all the additional hours he is forced to spend as a caterer every month just so he can cover rent. He knocks on the door.

"Enter!"

He enters.

"Morning, Cindy!"

Cindy's fervently typing away at her desktop. Her eyes are hidden behind a vibrant blue light reflecting off her reading glasses.

"Got your half and half right here." He sets her coffee down. "No sugar."

She says nothing, prompting him to briefly debate with himself as to whether he should ask about his assignment later. Then, as if sensing his gaze on her, she looks up from her computer at him, only to gesture lazily to the windowsill. Realizing what she wants him to do, he deflates.

Among the more degrading of his daily tasks is the watering of Cindy's bonsai tree. Her *fake* bonsai tree. He assumed that she'd been joking when she had first instructed him in its care.

But when no laughter followed the tutorial, he decided to just play along, believing that, if nothing else, it would show he was a team player. It hadn't worked.

After a reluctant spritzing, he moves back to stand across from her desk just as her printer whirs to life. "So, Cindy, I was hoping I could talk to you about something?"

"Did you pick up my dress?" she asks.

"About that," Napoleon pauses. "I had to take it back to the cleaners, but I've been assured it'll be ready before this evening."

"You do remember me telling you that tonight's one of the biggest nights of my career?"

"I do. Which is why I paid for it out of my pocket. Speaking of which, I was wondering if—"

"Here." She hands him a piece of paper, a credit card, and a key. "I need you to pick up all the things on this list and then drop them off at my apartment. Got it?"

"I . . . yes, of course."

"Be back by eleven."

Napoleon looks surprised. He glances down at the list, blinking hard as he double-checks the addresses.

"Uh, eleven?"

"Is that a problem?"

Shit yeah, it's a problem.

The addresses don't look to be anywhere near each other, *or* her place. Assuming that he wouldn't be waiting too long for the clerks to find whatever she ordered from their storage rooms, he'd still have to book it to the metro each time.

"No," he says, giving her his best fake smile. "No problem here."

"Good," she says curtly. "I've got a surprise for you this afternoon, and I don't want you to be late."

"Oh . . . Right, okay, I better get going then."

"If I find any taxi fees on my credit statement, your ass is grass, got it?"

"Understood."

"Drop that draft at the editor's desk on your way out," she says, gesturing to the pages in the printing tray as her attention returns to her monitor.

As he picks up the stack of paper, he notes the photo of an old man on the cover. It isn't someone Napoleon recognizes, but the headline isn't flattering: "Savant or screwball?"

He wants to keep reading, but he knows Cindy hates it when he reads her stuff in front of her. Besides, he's on a time crunch.

The next few hours fly by like a fighter jet as he races from the Epoch Tribune to a jewelry store in the Bronx to a boutique in Queens, back to an antique store in Manhattan before then finally, dropping everything off at her Fifth Avenue loft.

Halfway through the errands, Napoleon realizes that at his current rate of travel, he won't get back to the office until well into the afternoon. So, against his better judgment, he hails a cab and charges it to his already overdrawn bank account.

The elevator doors open on the main floor of the paper at 11:01 a.m.

"I'm here!" Napoleon says as he bolts into her office, breathing heavily. "I'm here! I made it!"

Cindy excuses herself from a conversation with Lena, the accountant.

"Congratulations," she says, guiding Napoleon out into the hall, "you can run errands. Now see that door over there. The one with the words *Storage Room* written on it?"

"Yeah?"

"That's the storage room. There's a stack of boxes in there that need to be sorted through and organized along the shelves."

"Boxes?"

"Yep. Boxes. Filled with old articles, company files, things like that. I want you to catalog and arrange them based on where their content fits best with the labels on the shelves. Got it? Great!"

Before he has a chance to respond, he's nudged forward out of her office, and the door's shut behind him with a finality that would rival death.

Not long after, during his afternoon of administrative hell, he checks his phone to find a text reminding him of the additional overdraft charge that's been added to his bank account.

Rage builds like bile inside him, and before he's aware of his actions, he's dialing a number.

***

Methicillin-resistant *Staphylococcus aureus*, or MRSA as it's often called, is a common strain of staph bacteria, which can cause infections in the body. It doesn't respond to many antibiotics, and if left untreated, it can be fatal—and also a huge pain in the ass to deal with at one in the morning if a hospital isn't an option. Apparently.

Not long after ending the call, the hitman's symptoms rose to debilitating levels. Having purged his stomach and flushed his system with enough water to drown a fish, he realizes he needed to use the phone again.

Every industry in the world has rules of engagement so common among its practitioners that they're considered clichés. Murder is no different.

Granted, these particular practitioners can't quite link up over lunch and complain about work in the same way as everyone else. But word of mouth is still a thing.

One such rule is that if you can handle a work emergency on your own, you do. If you can't, whoever you rely on better be ignorant or especially discreet. And qualified.

The prearranged knocking signal comes a little over two hours later. His "emergency contact," for lack of a better word, gets to work addressing his symptoms without asking a single question as to their origins.

Blood samples quickly reveal that he is suffering from toxic shock syndrome, and an obscure antibiotic is issued to keep him on his feet. After a few hours of sleep and several water bottles to replenish his hydration, he still doesn't feel great.

The coordinates provided by the client over the phone are for a geographical drop point that marks the location of a *Salix babylonica* in Central Park. The tree is situated on the edge of the lake between Wagner Cove and Bow Bridge, which are connected by a concrete path.

Further down the path to the right of the tree, there is a row of park benches. Several of them are being occupied by oblivious park goers. And one by the hitman.

As he pretends to look at his phone, he notes the potential hazards, blind spots, and escape routes out of his peripheries.

The timer on his watch beeps. It's noon. With nothing to deter him, he makes his move.

As he pushes the branches of the tree out of the way, he can't help being impressed by the client's choice of drop site. A thick layer of low-hanging foliage provides perfect cover from the park's prying eyes.

He notes the seemingly ordinary terrain beneath the trunk of the tree; grass, dirt, and a wooden log covered in mud is all that is present.

However, closer examination of the mud reveals that it's cool to the touch, and only appears to concentrate in thick clumps on the top half of the log.

Signs of worms and fungi are also evident.

Half a foot on the other side, the grass seems to abruptly change to a concave patch of mud the same size as the clumps on the log.

With a slight push, the log rolls back into the mud patch to reveal a folder hiding underneath. This added security step seems a tad unnecessary, if not a little paranoid. But the hitman doesn't dwell on it for very long.

His clients are by their very nature, eccentric.

He hits redial on his burner phone and waits until the call goes through. "Where are those business invoices?" he asks.

"Faxing them over now."

There are rotating codes for each day of the week.

"I—we think a witness has it," the voice says. "The file you've been provided should contain a brief overview of his employment history, address, physical description, etc."

"That'll cost you double." He walks back out from beneath the tree and onto the path.

"The deal was the engineer and the flash drive. As far as we're concerned, the terms have yet to be fulfilled."

"I was assured the item would be on their person."

"And our intel says that it was."

"Are you suggesting . . . an oversight?" He lets the weight of implication carry in his voice.

There is a pause on the other end.

"We're not wanting a full service, merely asset acquisition."

"And market infiltration."

"We're prepared to pay an additional fourth."

"Half," he says. "Money up front."

Another pause.

"Half."

The line goes dead.

Chapter 5

"Thanks for doing this."

Napoleon adjusts the tilt of his seat in her rusty Pontiac as they drive down the street. He glances out the window to see the midday sun is reflecting off the high-rises, creating the impression that it's everywhere at once. He also sees a woman struggling to remove a piece of trash that the wind's blown onto her face.

"It was on my way home," Skylar says bluntly, her focus fixed on the road ahead. There's a lit cigarette between the fingers of her hand as it rests on the steering wheel.

Wanting to chip away at the ice, Napoleon asks, "Grabbing something to eat before class?"

She gives him the side-eye. "Mm-hmm."

He sighs. "You're pissed."

"I'm not pissed."

"You are. You're pissed with me for doing this."

"I'm not—" She stops herself from yelling. "I think what you did was a noble thing. You instinctively ran to help that guy when you saw he was in trouble. That says something to me. But going back and asking to be compensated for that act of kindness? Well, that says something to me too."

Nervous, he picks at the lining of the door.

"Stop that."

"Sorry . . . If you don't like what I'm doing, why are you giving me a ride?"

She takes a drag on her cigarette. "I'm allowed to disagree with you and still want to support a friend."

He smiles. "You sap."

"I will leave you on the side of the road, I swear to God," she says, trying not to laugh.

He shifts in his seat and, in doing so, kicks some of the trash coating the floor of her car.

"You can just put some of that on the back seat."

"You've got a lot of shit down here."

"Yes, thanks for that. Just—"

"What is this?" he asks, picking up a branding iron shaped like a heart.

"That . . ." She pauses. There's a look on her face that suggests the gears in her head are spinning. "That is for the fireplace. I thought it would be . . . cuter," —the word seems to irritate her— "than getting one of the more classic looking pokers."

This is a lie.

"And these?" he asks, holding up a plastic bag full of bondage ties. "I'm assuming these also have something to do with poking?"

"Wow, that's amazing," she says, taking the bag from him and tossing it on the backseat. "I didn't realize you were a comedian as well as a hitchhiker."

"Actually, I called you, and you came and picked me up in your car. Technically, that makes you a cabbie."

She takes a second to reflect on his remark before flicking cigarette ash over his legs.

"Ah!" He begins frantically rubbing at his chinos. "What are you? Oh, hot, hot!"

She can't help but laugh.

It started with a sexual attraction. And after a week in bed together, they had discovered that they also liked each other. They decided not to get together, however, for fear that the expectations of a serious relationship would ruin their ability to crack jokes and communicate honestly.

So when new people came along, they supported each other. And when the new people inevitably broke things off because they supported each other, they offered each other a shoulder to lean on.

A short while later, they pull up outside the hospital. Even in daylight, the place has an inexplicable brutality to it that isn't softened by the knowledge that lives are being saved inside. It is one of those ugly certainties of life, like taxes, or forgetting login passwords.

"So," Skylar asks, "what's the plan?"

"No idea," he says. "Any advice?"

"This is unethical; don't do it."

"Okay . . . anything else?"

"Well, if I've learned anything from only sometimes attending my introduction to economics class, it's that the exchange of goods or services is orchestrated by what is known as a contract." She holds up two fingers, one on each hand. "Wherein two parties, both with something of value, come to a mutually beneficial decision to trade those things within an acceptable parameter of quantity, quality, and time."

"Right, but I don't have a contract with this guy. So what does that have to do with my situation?"

"Nothing." She shrugs. "But I've got a test in a week and could benefit from reviewing the material. How'd that sound by the way?"

Napoleon blinks several times before opening the door and exiting the car.

"Good luck!" she says as she pulls away.

He finds his way back to the reception area where he was the night before, only to be greeted by the distressing sounds of someone crying in a nearby room. Outside, a slender woman sits cross-legged, texting.

There's visible indifference on her face as though whatever is happening inside is of no concern to her.

The physician's assistant from the night before has since been replaced by a far less standoffish first point of contact. Unsure of what else to do, Napoleon decides the front desk is a good place to start.

"Hi," he says, approaching the receptionist. "I'm looking for . . . uh . . ."

What was his name again?

"Milo?" he asks. "Eadwulf, I think?"

"He's dead," comes a voice from behind him before the receptionist has a chance to respond.

He turns to see that the woman who was previously sat on her phone is now standing upright, her indifference replaced with a cold, calculating stare that is intensely focused on him. It's enough to send a chill down his spine.

"What?" he asks, having not fully absorbed what she said.

"He died this morning. Complications from surgery."

"That's . . . that's awful."

She leans her head a fraction to the left. Napoleon tries to suppress his discomfort, but his intuition is telling him she still picked up on it.

"Were you close?" she asks with a warmth that does not match her expression.

"I'm Napoleon Davis."

Why did you give your full name?

"I'm the guy who . . . who found him."

"Ah." She takes several steps toward him. "So you're who I have to thank for saving my brother's life."

Brother.

So this was Milo's sister.

He can't believe he didn't see it sooner; the resemblance is uncanny. Same black hair, same pale skin, same light, green eyes. They remind Napoleon of emeralds and, oddly, traffic lights.

Though where Milo's eyes had shown signs of anguish and fear, his sister's displayed the measured tranquility of power. They were also less bloodshot.

"My name's Adalyn," she says, the warmth in her voice growing stronger with every word. "If you don't mind me asking, what brings you here?"

"I, uh, I wanted to see how he was doing, you know, after everything."

She neither does nor says anything for several seconds. It's as if she was weighing every one of his words individually in her mind as she analyzed for inconsistencies, misplaced intonations, or general weakness.

"How noble," she says, her voice cutting through the cries he now identified as belonging to a woman.

He offers a nervous smile, and she responds by retrieving her phone from inside the jacket of her red pantsuit. A call is coming in on the other end. The first thing he notices after she answers is that the crying woman can now be heard both in re-al-time and through the phone.

"Wescott," Adalyn says, "see to it that Polli gets home safely when she's ready to leave. I'll be taking a friend to lunch."

Napoleon looks surprised. "Oh, I'm not sure if that's a—"

"Book a table for two at Podium for an hour from now. Two plates of the fusilli with sides of wild arugula and a couple of inferno cocktails, generous on the whisky."

"Very good, ma'am." Comes a voice through the receiver. "Shall I order you a car?"

"No, we'll take the metro."

"Understood."

Adalyn hangs up and offers Napoleon something in the realm of a flirtatious glance before walking off down the hall-way, leaving both him and the receptionist behind the desk in utter confusion.

What just happened?

She didn't believe his reasoning; he can glean that much. Lunch is likely her way of getting to the truth.

What he can't understand is why she'd be so interested. Did she think he was responsible for her brother's death? The no-tion disturbs him. A lot about her disturbed him. She seemed unaffected.

On the other hand, she's hot, and he's hungry. And with Milo dead, it looks like this fancy lunch is his best shot at re-solving the issue of the overdraft on his credit card.

Napoleon mutters to himself, "I can think of worst first dates."

***

It's times like these that Maggie really regrets getting a buzz cut. Her long hair would've made it much easier to avoid her boss's glaring irritation when she walked into the bistro a little after one in the afternoon. Thirty minutes after, technically.

"You're killing me, Maggie." He tosses her an apron.

"I know. Sorry, it won't happen again, I promise."

"What's your excuse this time? Family emergency? Car trouble?"

"If it's all the same to you, I'd rather not go into it."

"That has to be your laziest excuse yet." He gestures through the window at the curbside seating that makes up most of the bistro's back wall. "You're outside today, you got a few two-tops right now, and one single that's finishing up."

"I'm on it." She grabs a notepad as she runs out the door.

"Try and move some pies!" he yells. "They're going bad!"

The outdoor seating is made up of a portion of the street that was sequestered by a barrier of square-shaped pots filled with an assortment of flowers. A wooden awning shades most of the tables, but additional umbrellas are available for use at the patron's request.

Both two-tops are done with their meals by the time Maggie arrives. Try as she does to push the dessert menu, nobody bites, and eventually, she excuses herself from the small talk, offering assurances that the checks would be arriving momentarily.

Hopefully, the single table would be a different story.

"You look like a man who enjoys a slice of pie," she says, putting her best waitress foot forward.

A passing car honks just as the man responds. He's sitting alone in a faded T-shirt and dark sunglasses. Like her, his head is shaved. But where she'd opted for the "dismantle the pa-triarchy" aesthetic, he went for more of a traditional military look.

He had the build for it, as well as the posture. But there's a sickly green complexion to his skin that makes her wonder if he's dealing with an illness of some kind.

"What was that?" she asks.

He smiles as he says again, "Just the check is fine."

"Okay, you sure? I could put some cream on it. Bring out a nice latte as well?"

"How are you?"

"I'm sorry?"

"It's just I get the impression you need a win. And I'm won-dering why that is."

Thinking it's a joke, she laughs nervously. When he doesn't laugh back, her face turns red. "Oh, I'm . . . I'm fine. Really. It's nothing."

"Your eyes are puffy; it looks like you've been crying."

"My . . . I don't think that's any of your business."

"Is it a guy? I bet it's because of a guy."

"Now, look!" she says hotly, making everyone on the patio turn her way. "I haven't been crying, and even if I had, I'm not going to discuss my private life with an insensitive prick like you of all people, so would you back off?!"

"Sure." He smiles once more. "I'll just take the check."

"Coming right up."

Chapter 6

"Tell me about yourself, Napoleon."

A wordless metro ride, a plate of fusilli, and several cocktails later, Napoleon finds himself sitting across from Adalyn in the nicest restaurant he's ever patronized. The afternoon forecast shows strong signs of a food coma with a possibility of inebriation.

Adalyn, however, appears unfazed by the drinks, the meal, or his attempts at witty repartee. Although he reckons the acute case of slurred speech he is presently suffering from probably isn't helping.

He swallows a mouthful. "Well, I'm a college dropout, working part-time at night to cover the bills and full-time at a newspaper during the day to try and jump-start my career in journalism."

"What newspaper?" she asks.

"The Tribune."

The faintest hint of surprise tickles her face. "So . . . you're a colleague of Cindy Li's then?"

"I wouldn't say colleague. More of a trainee than anything."

"I imagine you wouldn't be for very long if you landed a story."

"That's the idea." He sighs. "I was hoping to get my first assignment today actually, but I guess I haven't proven myself yet."

"How does one prove themselves a journalist without writing anything?" she asks, genuinely bemused.

"It's very political. You see, the newspaper is renowned, and not everyone gets a chance to look behind the curtain. I'm very lucky in a lot of ways to just have the chance to . . . run errands . . . for people who actually work there."

The ridiculousness of how it sounds dawns on him as he says it out loud. Where that speech even came from is a mystery. Though, if he had to guess, it was probably a marketing campaign of some kind.

"What about you?" he asks, not wanting to talk about himself any longer. "How are you doing, considering—"

"I've done what I can to leverage my connections at all the various publications around town so that we have time to process everything before the inevitable media storm. At most, I've bought us a day or two . . . the police have opened a homicide investigation."

"Couple gunshots to the chest? Seems a likely conclusion."

That was terse.

"Not to mention the bruising."

Napoleon's eyes drop at her mention of the bruising, prompting her to ask: "You have a different theory?"

"I don't know." He taps a finger against the table. "I'm not an expert, but the color of his bruises made me wonder if maybe he hadn't picked them up earlier."

"You're suggesting he was beaten first and shot later on?"

He bites his tongue. The taste of blood immediately replaces remnants of the fusilli. For someone having lunch with a woman who thinks he had a hand in the death of her brother, he isn't doing a good job of disproving that suspicion.

Damn you, whisky.

"That'd be my theory," he says.

"Is there anything you can tell me about that night?" she asks. "Anything that stuck out to you as strange?"

"Besides finding a dead body?"

"Did he say anything to you? Anything that we might be able to use to find out who did this to him? Or why?"

He shakes his head. "He'd lost a lot of blood. He was pretty much inaudible by the time I got there."

She nods.

He decided to leave out the part about Milo calling him a cocksucker. It felt pretty innocuous in the grand scheme of things, and he's already feeling as if he's stepped in it a handful of times since they sat down.

Besides, it would be a definitive mood killer.

He's about to propose they look at the dessert menu when she gets a text and checks her phone.

"My apologies," she says, "I have to get back to work."

"Oh . . . no worries."

"Do you have plans this evening?"

"Uh, I've got a shift at the—"

"Can you cancel it?"

"Cancel?"

"There's a gala downtown," she says. "It's a charity event for the preservation of the endangered *Bombus*."

"What's a *Bombus*?"

"It's the scientific term for a bumblebee. Do you own a tuxedo?"

"No."

"I'll have one sent around with Wescott and the car." She fires off a text. "Let's say eightish?"

"Ish?"

She's already getting up from the table.

"Hang on, stop," he says, his voice a higher pitch than he wanted. "I appreciate the invitation, and I'm flattered. Really. You're very pretty and clearly quite an accomplished—"

"This isn't a date, Napoleon."

". . . It isn't?"

"Every member of my family will be at this gala." She puts on her jacket. "I'd like to hire you to investigate them."

"You think one of them killed Milo?" he asks rhetorically.

"Or paid someone to do it. I can't be sure, and I can't be seen snooping around in case they get spooked and try to run."

"Why me?"

"You're unassuming."

Ouch.

"And you have an eye for detail as well as a believable reason for being there."

"Which is?"

"They're all very keen to meet the man who saved Milo's life." She chuckles. "If only for a few more hours."

He isn't sure why, but he chuckles back. "I don't know. This all sounds kind of dangerous, not to mention a little awkward. Besides, I can't—did you say, 'hire me'?"

"I'm prepared to offer you $10,000," she says so offhandedly it could've been a sock.

"Ten thou—thou—thou—"

"I take it we have a deal?"

Before he can respond, his phone rings. Cindy's calling. He's hit with the sudden and horrifying realization that his thirty-minute lunch break ended nearly two hours ago.

"Napoleon, where the hell are you?! You're missing Lena's surprise party, and we're out of plastic cups!"

He puts his free hand to his forehead. "Uh, that's why I'm not there actually. I got sent out for cups."

Adalyn pushes out her bottom lip as though impressed with how fast he's able to think on his feet.

"Well, hurry back, dammit!" Cindy's voice booms. "One of the junior writers brought in homemade punch, and people are getting antsy!"

"Yep, I'm on my way back now." He hangs up as he turns to Adalyn. "Can I think about it?"

"Wescott will be outside your apartment at eight o'clock, the offer expires at 8:05 p.m. You needn't concern yourself with the bill; they've already put everything on my tab."

With that, she's gone. He considers whistling but doesn't. Not long after, the waiter appears, prompting him to grin.

"I'll do another Inferno," he says, shaking his empty glass. "To go, if possible."

***

The address in the folder is for a second-story apartment in a three-story Brooklyn walk-up. From the street, he notes the decrepit front door, which windows are accessible by fire escape, and the quickest path back to his hatchback.

He familiarized himself with some rudimentary information about the apartment's floor plan, the three inhabitants, and their daily schedules.

Napoleon Davis, the alleged witness to Milo Eadwulf's death, is presently at an internship across town. James Miller is scheduled to leave in ten minutes. And Skylar Lewis has a college lecture.

Ideally, he would find the flash drive in the apartment. If not, he would plant a bug that would wirelessly transmit to a monitor in his car, allowing him to see and hear their every conversation.

A proverbial ace in the peephole.

While he's more than capable of getting in and out of the place without being detected, his plan involves leaving signs of a break-in: shattered plates, broken cabinets, overturned furniture.

In his experience, these were effective tools for answering questions. Questions like why has this happened? What did the burglar want? Were they successful in getting it?

He couldn't afford to spend hours listening to them babble on irrelevantly after all.

A short while later, James Miller, alias Burger, walks out of the building wearing a neon traffic vest, steel toe boots, and other clothes.

As Miller heads up the street to the metro line, the man exits the hatchback and heads for the building, his cap kept low over his eyes with a hoodie hanging lazily over the top.

The goal is to seem inconspicuous. His face needs to be concealed from the security cameras placed around the building. His body language needs to come across relaxed.

Given the opportunity, he'd steal the security footage of his visit from the front desk on his way out, but it didn't pay to rely on that alone.

A couple carrying grocery bags unlock the building's main entrance as he approaches from behind. Ironically, they're so locked in conversation that they're oblivious to him walking in just as the door closes behind them. To put some distance between him and them, he idles near the mailboxes briefly while they climb the stairs.

When their chatting fades to a muted muffle, he follows up after them. According to the floor plan, the apartment he's looking for will be the first door off the stairs on the second story.

To avoid looking suspicious, he refrains from putting his head on a swivel as he removes a set of lock picks from his pocket. Surprisingly, the door isn't locked; Miller must have forgotten on his way out.

Footsteps descending the stairs spur him forward, prompting a quick and skillful substitution of the lockpicks in his hands for the gun in his belt loop.

A quick scan of the apartment reveals three things. The first is that although it's a two-bedroom apartment, a corner of the living room has been sectioned off as a third sleeping quarter.

The second is that the place is tacky. Really tacky. The furniture appears to have been sourced either from the dumpsters or the things heading there.

But the third thing serves to answer why Miller left the front door unlocked.

The blinds are drawn. The TV's on, and a rom-com couple looks to be having their meet-cute. A lit cigarette resides in the tray on the coffee table.

She has a spoon halfway up to her wide-open mouth in one hand and a bowl of cereal in the other. Milk drips off the spoon and onto her pajamas as she blinks at him from the couch.

He draws the gun—to instill fear more than invoke death. He still needs to avoid linking two crime scenes with a murder weapon, if at all possible.

Of all the days to skip class. She doesn't scream. The paralysis brought on by a stranger with a gun is too debilitating. He sighs as he slowly shuts the door.

It always is.

Chapter 7

The Epoch Tribune's break room is in complete disarray by the time Napoleon arrives back at the office. Crumbs, plates of half-eaten cake, and used napkins litter every available surface. Space has seemingly been created so that partygoers would have room to dance.

Judging from the few remaining drunk stragglers, however, the party's long since ended.

"Finally," Cindy says, getting up from the table that she was sitting on next to Lena. "Where the fuck . . . have you been?"

For someone who supposedly has the biggest event of her career that evening, Cindy is doing a remarkable job of making sure intoxication will be her plus one.

"I brought cups," he says, holding up a bag he picked up from the bodega on his way over.

Fast blinking and a furrowed brow suggest she's struggling to put them in focus as she approaches. She shakes her head like she's trying to either throw off her buzz or convey her disappointment.

"Does it look like we need cups?" she says with a hiccup while gesturing to the room.

So it is to be disappointment.

"Well, no, but you asked me to—"

"We found pencil holders." She grins triumphantly. "Ones that weren't made from wire mesh. The punch kind of tasted like pencil lead, but poisoning aside, it's a rather delightful garnish."

"Resourceful." He tries to mask his irritation at having to pay for a work-related item on his overdrawn credit card. Again.

"Yeah . . ." she says, smiling as she glances around the room. "Clean this up."

"Beg your pardon?"

"You heard me. The whole room. Not just the trash either. I want all the furniture put back where it was before as well." She pats his cheek on her way past. "When you're done with that bring some coffee and aspirin to my office. I feel like I stuck my head in front of a fire hydrant."

Maybe it's the booze. Maybe it's the unending stream of bullshit he's got to deal with daily. Or maybe it's that he's already been offered compensation to do the job that he thought he would've been learning how to do by now already.

Whatever the reason, something snaps in Napoleon's brain at that moment, and before he's even aware of the words coming out of his mouth, he shouts:

"I quit!"

"Quit?" Cindy turns back toward him. "Who's quitting?"

"I am. I did not sign up to be the goddamn janitor or your personal gopher."

"Gopher?"

"Yeah, *go for* this Napoleon. *Go for* that Napoleon. Well, *go* fuck yourself, Cindy! I don't need this!"

"Is that right?" He makes to leave as she adds, "What are you going to do, kid?! You're a twenty-five-year-old dropout with no money and no connections. You've got nothing! I was the timber bridge across your river of despair, and you just dropped a match on my support beams." Her eyes go wide. "Someone write that down for me. Wait!"

For some reason, Napoleon turns around.

"What about my dress?" she asks, the desperation mounting in her voice.

With a grimace, he pulls the receipt he'd been issued for her dry cleaning out of his pocket and lets it drop onto the floor. Then turns out and walks out without looking back.

He smiles the whole metro ride home.

The first thing he notices when he walks into his apartment is that the shower's running. Even though the bathroom door is closed, the sound is unmistakable. Something is missing from the ensemble, however.

Before he can arrive at anything resembling a conclusion, he's grabbed from behind and placed in a sleeper hold. When he wakes, he finds himself tied to a chair at his kitchen table. He's lost most of the feeling in his hands; whatever material was used to restrain him is cutting into his wrists.

Sitting across from him on his left is a man with fresh scars on his face. Napoleon can see a silenced pistol sitting over on the kitchen counter.

"Who are you?" Napoleon asks.

The man answers with a right fist to his jaw.

"What are you doing back from work?" the man asks in return.

Napoleon spits out blood onto the floor. A tooth feels loose in his mouth, but his jaw still seems intact. He chuckles with a confidence that surprises even him.

"When are we going to stop playing who, what, when, where, and why?"

He's hit again.

"Where is it?" the man asks.

Guess we're still playing then.

"Why do you think I have it?"

He has no idea what the man is referring to, but he had done enough improv in college to know when to let a scene play out.

"Because Eadwulf didn't. It wasn't in his possessions, and it's not in this apartment, which means you either have it or you know where it is."

So this was Milo's killer. Despite the ringing in his ears and pain in his jaw, it's good to know his processing speeds haven't been affected. He tries to piece the information together.

He found Milo in an alley. Near a bus stop. Therefore, it's safe to assume he might've been leaving town. And trying to do so without alerting anyone by way of passport activity.

Ergo, the bus.

But people traveling, even if they were on the run, often had a suitcase with them. Or at the very least, a backpack. There'd been nothing like that around Milo when Napoleon found him. So this hitman could have taken it, assuming incorrectly, that whatever "it" was, would be inside.

But it hadn't been. What does that tell him? Not much, except that it is probably of a certain size. Probably portable.

It's a gamble, but if he can convince this guy that he knows what the item is by hinting at its dimensions, he might be willing to divulge more about its nature.

Having quit the internship, Napoleon decided on the metro home to accept Adalyn's offer of ten grand in exchange for his help in finding her brother's killer. The inside scoop on a high-profile murder story would surely do wonders for his career.

Oh, and it's the right thing to do.

Fortunately, it's already proving to be an easier task than he'd anticipated.

"He could've been carrying it!" he shouts, feigning anger to try and keep the man talking. "You should've searched Milo after you shot him, you amateur!"

A third punch connects with his cheekbone, opening the skin.

"He was searched," says the hitman, "but he was smart, and finding it merited a longer search than I had time to conduct. Then he gave it to you."

"What could I possibly gain from having it?"

"Don't play dumb. I know you're a journalist. All you believe in is sharing information."

"Technically, I was an intern." He tries to reposition his wrists in his restraints. "And we only believe in sharing *valuable* information."

The hitman laughs. "If you don't think whatever's on that flash drive is valuable, you're dumber than you look. Why would someone hire me to retrieve it if it wasn't worth something?"

There it is.

"Oh, I dunno. Maybe you're the nephew of some big player in the criminal underworld? Nepotism's pretty rampant in most industries these days."

"You're funny . . . I'm going to break your finger now."

"Woah, wait, just hang on a second!"

The hitman snaps the middle finger on Napoleon's left hand. Napoleon cries out in pain.

"Where is it, Mr. Davis?"

"The hospital could have it, genius! Ever think about that?!"

"They don't."

That was telling.

Surely, the hospital would've returned everything they'd found on Milo's person to his emergency contact when he died. So the fact that the hitman could say with certainty that the flash drive hadn't been returned, suggested Adalyn's theory was correct: Milo was killed by someone close to him.

The obvious suspect is his wife, Polli. It's always the wife. At least, it is in movies. She is more than likely his emergency contact, and she was the first one to arrive at the hospital after he was admitted.

But if it was that obvious, Adalyn wouldn't have needed his help in figuring it out and he also can't rule out the possibility that this hitman might have managed to gain access to Eadwulf's medical records.

All it would take is a computer hacker or an inside man at the hospital who's willing to pass along information. For all he knows, the hitman could have both.

Maybe it was that physician's assistant.

"Hate to break it to you, pal," Napoleon says, "but I don't have it on me. Now that doesn't mean I can't take you to it."

The hitman leans forward and puts his elbow on the table.

"Let's look at this situation from an economic standpoint," Napoleon says as he straightens up in his chair. "I have something of value to you. At the same time, you have something of value to me."

"I follow you so far."

"Glad to hear it. Now, if you kill me, you'll never find out where it's hidden. But if I die . . . well, that'll suck. The way I see it, we have a shared interest in coming to a mutually beneficial solution. Wouldn't you agree?"

The hitman leans back in his chair to stare at the ceiling. "I don't think I do. You see, the thing is, you've assumed we're in a stalemate. That I only have one option and it requires that I let you live . . . But you don't live alone, do you?" He gestures to the bathroom door. "I could hurt your friends. Could make you watch as they died. It would happen gradually. Over several hours. Days. Weeks."

Napoleon's face grows serious as the hitman continues, "And afterward, if you still didn't feel like talking, I would start on you. I'd use every trick in my book: insects, waterboarding—not fire, I'm not a monster—but skinning?"

He takes out a large dagger from the inside of his hoodie and makes a point of illustrating how sharp it is by tapping a finger along the edge briefly before dramatically pulling it away.

"So I'll ask you again. And make no mistake this will be the last time I ask nicely. Where is it?"

Before Napoleon can respond, the sound of a gun cocking pulls their attention to the other side of the kitchen. Standing by the now open front door, the hitman's silenced pistol in hand is James Miller.

"Burger!" Napoleon looks overjoyed.

His relief is short-lived, however, as the hitman then moves with shocking speed to reposition himself so that Napoleon is functioning as a human shield, the blade pressed against his carotid artery.

"Who's your friend, Napo?" Burger asks, gun at the ready.

"Come any closer and he dies," the hitman says.

"He dies, and you die."

The hitman smiles. "Ever killed someone before, *Burger*?"

"All the time. My KD ratio is fucking toppers."

Napoleon knows that Burger's talking about video games, but he isn't going to be the one to clarify that on the off chance that the hitman didn't understand.

"This isn't a video game, kid."

Damn.

"There are no restarts here. If you pull that trigger, you might hit me. Then again, you might hit Napo too. Or, you could miss both of us and hit a straggler, like her." He gestures at the door.

"Burger don't!" Napoleon shouts.

Too late. The brief turn of Burger's head gives the hitman time to vault across the living room and out the single-paned glass window before plummeting two stories to the sidewalk below. The window with the fire escape is, unfortunately, in the bathroom.

Shards of glass slice across his arms as he falls. Despite tucking and rolling, he fractures his foot as he hits the concrete.

Burger rushes to the window and opens fire. Bullets wiz past the hitman as he races up the street in a desperate flee for cover.

Before he can reach safety, he's hit. It's not fatal but it's created another wound in his shoulder. Seconds later, he disappears into an alley and out of range of the gunfire.

"He's gone," Burger says, turning back to Napoleon. "Boy, I guess it's a good thing, I forgot my lunch."

"Can I get a little help?" Napoleon asks, unable to loosen the restraints tying him to the chair.

"Sure, I—Son of a bitch!"

"What, what was it?"

"That fuck used my fishing lines to tie you down. Does he have any idea how much this stuff costs?!"

"Would you please just untie me? I can't feel my hands."

"All right, all right."

Burger retrieves a pair of scissors from one of the kitchen drawers before delicately beginning to cut through the wire between Napoleon's hands.

"Thanks," Napoleon says, rubbing his wrists, and trying not to touch his broken finger against anything. "I owe you one."

"Don't mention it. Who was that asshole?"

"The guy who shot the other guy I tried to help the other night. He was looking for something. A flash drive."

"What's a flash drive?"

"It's a hardware interface."

Burger stares at him blankly.

"Sometimes referred to as a universal serial bus?"

Still no response.

"It's like a portable storage device for your computer."

"Why couldn't you just say that?"

Napoleon sighs before switching on the kitchen faucet and running his wrists under the cold water.

"He left our shower running too?" Burger asks, noticing the sound of running water still emanating from the bathroom.

"I swear to God, if either of you thinks I'm paying the bill this month, I'm gonna—" He screams.

Startled, Napoleon turns and barely manages to catch himself against the counter before his legs give out.

That unidentifiable thing that felt like it was missing when he first walked into the apartment suddenly becomes clear to him: whenever Burger uses the shower, he likes to sing. He isn't any good, but he does sing loud enough that he can be heard from anywhere in the apartment.

Skylar, on the other hand, can sing but rarely does and never when she thinks someone else is listening.

She also preferred baths.

Chapter 8

"He jumped out the window?"

Sitting across from Napoleon and James, Cayden makes note of the vacant expressions on their teary faces. As a detective, he knows that look all too well.

The way tragedy seared into the psyche was universal.

The team had arrived to find the body of Skylar Lewis, lying in the shower with her neck hanging over the rim of the bath at a contorted angle.

Napoleon and James were initially questioned separately to ensure that their stories lined up. Creative liberties aside, they both managed to walk the detectives through a consistent recap of the events that led to them finding the body.

Mr. Davis had allegedly been forced to restrain Mr. Miller to prevent him from moving her into a more decent position, which would have compromised the crime scene. For his trouble, he'd taken a punch to his already bruised face.

When things checked out, they were allowed to regroup, whereupon another round of questioning began. Protocol didn't necessarily demand that they do this, but Douglas had insisted. As far as Douglas is concerned, it's the second time in two days that a POI in a homicide investigation had been found at a crime scene.

He'd already taken Cayden aside to discuss his theory as to what had occurred:

1. Davis and Lewis have a domestic argument,
2. Davis loses the argument and gets angry,

3. Davis comes up with a revenge plan,
4. Davis quits his job where he makes no money – giving him a legitimate reason for deviating from his schedule and being home in the middle of the day,
5. Davis enters his apartment disguised as the hitman,
6. Davis kills Lewis and sets it up to look like an accident,
7. Davis exits the apartment via the fire escape, so he doesn't appear to be leaving on the security footage,
8. Davis re-enters the apartment as himself,
9. James Miller, Davis's accomplice, returns having "forgotten his lunch",
10. Together they wipe down the bathroom removing Davis's prints,
11. Miller then ties Davis to the chair and beats him, which explains the bruise on Miller's hand and the cuts on Davis's face,
12. They throw something out the window and fire a couple of rounds into the street to substantiate their story of how hitman escaped,

Cayden had immediately had questions:

1. What were they arguing about?
2. How does this relate to Milo Eadwulf?
3. How do you account for Davis being at lunch at Podium across town at the same time the security footage has him allegedly entering the apartment dressed as the hitman?
4. How do you account for him quitting his job at the

same time as Lewis's alleged time of death based on the initial forensics ruling?

5. Why would Davis give a witness statement that claims Lewis preferred having baths over showers and then set it up to look like she slipped and fell in the shower?

6. Why would Miller agree to help Davis kill Lewis?

7. Where'd they get the gun? If the hitman didn't jump out the window, did they throw it out?

8. And why are there traces of blood on the glass shards?

It had been nearly five hours. Suffice to say, they were starting to fall short of productive. Forensics was finishing up, and the witnesses were growing less cooperative since they'd been advised not to leave town while the case was still ongoing.

"And took off east," Napoleon says, notably irritated. "James fired six shots from the window using the man's gun but only hit him once in the left shoulder."

"And who discovered the body?" Cayden asks, looking up from his notepad.

Burger glares at him. "Her name was Skylar."

"Skylar, of course," he says, trying to deescalate the tension. "Who found Skylar in the shower?"

"After the hitman escaped, James untied me and went to see why the shower was running. I heard him scream and turned to . . ." Napoleon takes a second to collect himself. "We've already been over this."

"We're almost done. In your initial statement, you said something felt off to you about the apartment when you walked in?"

"I didn't realize it at the time but, usually, if the shower is running, I hear James singing."

Burger's knee bounces against the ground. "You got any leads on this guy?"

"We're not at liberty to discuss open investigations."

"Not at liberty to discuss? That prick killed my—"

"James."

"You said he was looking for a flash drive, is that right?"

"Yeah," Napoleon says. "He seemed to be under the impression Milo gave it to me before he died."

"Did he?" Douglas asks. It's the first time he's said anything to him or Burger directly.

"No."

"You're sure?"

"Yes, I'm sure."

"Who gives a shit about a flash driver?!" Burger shouts. "My best friend is dead, and her killer's still out there!"

Cayden puts up a hand. "Sir, I need you to calm down."

"She could've slipped in the shower," Douglas chirps.

"Hill!"

"Were you not listening?" Burger's eyes shift to Douglas. "And how do you explain the window then, genius?" He gestures to Napoleon. "Or his fucked-up face?"

"Genetics," Douglas mutters.

Seeing red, Burger makes a motion to stand up, but Napoleon puts a hand on his shoulder to dissuade him.

He knows what Burger's thinking.

He also knows that acting on this impulse will likely go over about as well as a fart in a scuba suit.

"Alright, let's everyone just relax for a second here," Cayden says. He's then hit with a raspy coughing fit.

"Mr. Miller," he says after it subsides. "I understand how the two of you must be feeling."

"Do you now?"

"But even with the hallway footage from the security tapes, we still haven't established anything that *definitively* solidifies the suspect you've described as the one responsible for Ms. Lewis's death."

"He was scratched."

"What was that?" Cayden turns toward Napoleon.

"His face had several open cuts on it. The first thing he asked me was what I was doing home from work, which means, he knew my work schedule. Therefore, he likely knew all of our schedules. And since no one's usually home at this point in the day, he must have figured now would be the best possible time to break in and search for the flash drive. Only . . . only Skylar skipped class."

A new batch of tears wells up in his eyes before joining the dry blood on his cheek. He wipes them away quickly.

"He knew her death would have to be ruled as an accident if he was going to cover his tracks. So he made it seem like she'd slipped in the shower and broken her neck. At least, that's what I would've thought if I'd come home when I typically do."

The very notion of the hitman trying to manipulate him like this provokes anger in Napoleon. "Except I quit my job today," he adds. "And if James hadn't shown up when he did, I would have been killed, the hitman would have disappeared, and neither of you would have a clue how not one, not two, but three people really died."

Douglas is fuming. "You arrogant—"

Cayden cuts him off. "And the scratches?"

"She didn't go down without a fight. Check under her nails. My guess is you'll find traces of blood."

There's a brief pause.

"Forensics!" Cayden shouts.

"Yeah?" comes a voice from the bathroom.

"You find any blood under Ms. Lewis's fingernails?"

The faint sounds of intelligent murmurings and clinking beakers can be heard before that same voice shouts:

"Yeah!"

Cayden shoots a look at Douglas. Douglas shrugs.

Cayden turns back to both roommates. "We'll look into it."

"Let's pack it up!" Douglas yells.

"Yeah," Burger cheers as the cops begin filing out the door. "Damn right you'll look into it! Hey, let us know if you need any more help, okay? It's only your job, right? Who says you have to be good at that?!" When the last of them have piled out into the hallway, he slams the door, turns, and smacks Napoleon on his shoulder. "That was badass!"

"Ow! Would you quit hitting me?"

"My bad, seriously though." He's grinning from ear to ear. "You pulled that genius card straight out of your back pocket and set it down like—" He pretends to throw an imaginary card down on an imaginary table: "Blackjack bitches!"

Napoleon chuckles appreciatively before suddenly growing very serious. At first, Burger thinks he might be having a stroke.

"What are you . . . what's happening?"

Without a word, Napoleon walks past him and out into the hall, almost as if he's in a trance.

It takes the thoroughly confused Burger a minute to collect himself before he follows Napoleon out into the hall.

"Hey!" he shouts down the stairs at him. "Where are you going?"

"I'll be back," Napoleon says without looking up. "Just need to check something."

"This isn't some kind of mental breakdown, is it?!"

"No!"

"Are you sure?"

"No!"

On the street outside the front of the building, a group of journalists has gathered to get statements on what happened from the police, and several of the more willing tenants.

It quickly becomes apparent to the journalists, however, that the tenants can provide little in the way of color beyond such classic lines as: "I heard gunshots," and "This whole neighborhood's gone to shit."

Their focus shifts predominantly to the police, specifically Douglas Hill, who's in the process of giving a quick recap of the situation when he spots Napoleon loitering just inside the door to his apartment building.

Napoleon, whose plan had been to wait until the crowd had dispersed before venturing outside, suddenly finds himself needing to adapt on the fly as Douglas gestures his way.

He mouths something Napoleon can't hear but is quickly able to decipher when all the journalists, sensing a fresh angle, turn his way.

What a prick.

The last of the police cars drive off as he steps out onto the street to be bombarded with questions:

"Mr. Davis, how do you feel after having been attacked?"

"Were you scared, Mr. Davis?!"

"Are you sad to have lost your friend, Ms. Lewis?"

"Do you think the police will catch the man who did this?"

"Do you blame yourself, Mr. Davis?"

"Aaaaaahhhh!"

It's three blocks to the dry cleaners, but he barely registers any of the run. He's too preoccupied with the three thoughts continuously circulating in his head.

Skylar's dead; it's all my fault; I pulled it out of my back pocket.

Skylar's dead; it's all my fault; I pulled it out of my back pocket.

Skylar's dead; it's all my fault; I pulled it out of my—

DING! The old school shopkeeper's bell rings out through the dry cleaners as he pulls the door open, prompting the overweight Albanian gentleman behind the desk to say, "Welcome to—"

"Hi," Napoleon interjects. "I was in here last night and dropped off a dress that I was told would be ready by this afternoon?"

"Do you have the receipt?"

"Yes." He fumbles through his pockets. "No, shit, I lost it."

"That's fine, sir. As long as it's under your account." The Albanian man cracks his fingers before then dangling them over the keyboard of the nineties-style desktop sitting on the counter in front of him. "Can I have your name?"

"Ah, right, so, funny story, the account is under my boss's name. I was picking it up for her you see and—"

"I'm sorry, sir." It's the Albanian's turn to interject. "But if the item isn't in your account and you don't have the receipt there's nothing I can—"

They hear her approach before they see her.

"Идиот! Это забавный мальчик, о котором я говорил вчера вечером. Ты никогда меня не слушаешь!"

She sets the dress down on the counter before turning to smack the Albanian across the chest.

"Это даже не вопрос! Вы просто отключите все, что это не футбол или открытие пивной банки! Кстати, у нас на обед Солянка!"

As fast as she comes, she goes, leaving only the dress and an awkward silence in her wake.

Flummoxed, Napoleon opts for a casual scratching at the back of his head before pointing at the dress and offering up the smoothest remark he can think of:

"So, I'm gonna go."

"Thank you very much for your business," replies the Albanian man without missing a beat.

"No, yeah, any time. Thank you for your career choice."

"Yeah . . . okay."

After exiting the cleaners and taking a minute to cringe at his inability to converse with others, Napoleon begins tearing the dress out from its protective layer of plastic.

It all comes down to a theory. A theory that hinges on his intuition. If he's wrong, he'll be at a dead end.

The thought alone is enough to make him laugh, cry, and rage all at once but just as he's beginning to think that he's reached rock bottom, a homeless man wanders past and shouts, "Been there, bud!"

Aw man . . . Big day.

Chapter 9

The evening sun shines in through the shattered windowpane. It's accompanied by the distant sounds of traffic and pedestrians on the street below.

Someone shouts, "Get out of the road!"

Someone answers, "Your mother should've swallowed you!"

There's a draft wreaking havoc on all the lightweight items strewn about the living room. One such item is Burger's drink napkin, which he's taken to holding onto whenever he wants to take a swig from his beer.

After a toast in Skylar's honor, he and Napoleon plopped down in the living room and are currently staring at the flash drive on the coffee table.

After another minute of mournful silence, Burger picks it up to examine it more closely. "You know, I had no idea dresses came with pockets," he says.

"That's your big takeaway?"

"It just surprising is all."

"Irrelevant is what it is."

Burger sniffs the air, picks up a funny smell, and tracks its origin to the flash drive.

"Jesus," he says, pulling away from it in disgust. "It stinks of shit. What kind of flash drive smells like asshole?"

Napoleon stifles a laugh. He had asked himself the same question upon finding it in the pocket of Cindy's dress outside of the dry cleaners. It hadn't taken long to come up with an explanation.

"Well," he says, "the hitman did say Milo hid it where no one would find."

Burger's eyes go wide. "You mean?"

Napoleon nods.

"Oh, what the fuck!"

He drops the flash drive and furiously begins wiping his hands on his pants as Napoleon rises to grab a box of disinfectant wipes from the kitchen. After removing one for himself, he tosses the box to Burger.

"It's incredible," he says as he picks the flash drive up and wipes it down.

"How's a shit-covered flash drive incredible?" Burger asks, scrubbing his hands.

"Not the drive, Milo. Think about it. He had to have been down several quarts of blood when I found him. He was probably in a ton of pain and barely conscious, and yet he was cognizant enough to discern that I was not only holding a dress but also that it had pockets. For him to have been able to move the drive into one of those pockets without me realizing it, given the motor functions, he likely had at the time? I'm guessing the hitman was right; this guy was probably a genius."

Burger reaches over and takes the flash drive from his hands. "So what do you think is on it?"

"No idea." Napoleon shrugs. "Could be anything."

"Should we find out?"

Napoleon takes it back from Burger. "People are willing to kill for this thing. Whatever's on it must be incredibly valuable to someone. Knowing the truth would likely put us in danger."

"So . . . should we find out?"

"Yeah, fuck it, why not?"

As they rise to their feet, in search of a laptop, there's a knock at the front door. KNOCK, KNOCK, KNOCK.

They both freeze for several seconds until Napoleon asks, "What do we do?"

Burger responds by picking up a lamp and taking up a fighting stance. For want of a better idea, Napoleon follows his lead and scans around frantically for a weapon. Eventually, his eyes fall over the box of disinfectant wipes just as there's another knock at the door. KNOCK, KNOCK, KNOCK.

Armed to the dentures, they quietly make their way over to stand on either side of the peephole, whereupon Burger starts signaling instructions to Napoleon with his hands. They are long and incomprehensible and accomplish little more than to confuse Napoleon and frustrate Burger.

KNOCK, KNOCK, KNOCK.

"Who is it?" Napoleon asks.

"Wescott, sir. Adalyn Eadwulf's driver? I've been instructed to take you to the gala this evening."

"Shit! I totally forgot."

"Gala?" Burger asks. "What's he talking about? Why do you have so many new friends all of sudden?"

"I got invited to this thing earlier by Milo's sister, and she said she'd send a car round to—" Napoleon drops the wet wipes in shock.

"You all right?" Burger asks. "You look like you just realized you have to go to Times Square."

"Are you nearly ready, sir?" Wescott asks through the door.

"Yeah, just gimme a second would you, pal?" Napoleon leads Burger farther away from the door before whispering, "It's Milo's sister. She hired the hitman."

"What? How do you know?"

"We got lunch earlier, and she said she was going to send a car around here to pick me up. But I never gave her our address."

"She must've had it already," Burger says, putting the pieces together. "And she was trying to keep you away while the guy searched the place."

"He was probably planning to leave without us ever knowing he'd been here."

"But Skylar was home," Burger says, clenching his fist so hard the lamp in his hand shatters.

"Sir," comes Wescott's voice through the door. "I have only been instructed to wait until—"

"Yeah okay, just hang on one second!" Napoleon shouts before turning to Burger. "I'm going to go."

"Have you lost your mind?!" Burger asks in a whispered shout.

"We need evidence and right now we have the upper hand. She doesn't know that we know that she's the killer. Plus, we have this." He holds up the flash drive.

"Then I'm going too."

Napoleon shakes his head. "Too suspicious. Besides, my guess is she only rented one tux."

"Fine." He grabs the flash drive. "Then I'm taking this."

"What?"

"I'm not about to let you walk into the wolf's den with our only leverage over the enemy. What if she searches you? There'd be nothing to stop her from taking it, killing you, and dumping your body in a vat of acid."

"Acid?"

"Rich people have acid! Look, I'll take it somewhere and hide until you get back. Then, based on what you find, we'll plan our next move."

"You don't have to do that. If I hadn't agreed to lunch with her, maybe none of this would've happened. This is my mess to clean up."

"That bitch killed my roommate. Burger ain't the type to let that shit slide. Plus, if you die, there's no one to help me with utilities."

Napoleon nods.

"Sir," Wescott says, "it's 8:04 p.m."

"I'm coming, I'm coming."

He opens the door to reveal a man in his mid-forties in a black suit, white shirt, black tie, and a chauffeur's hat. His expression is stern. His posture, rigid. His hair, graying.

"Wow," Napoleon says. "You were made for this job, weren't you?"

"It was this or a surfing instructor, sir. Shall we be off?"

"Lead the way, pal."

***

The second Napoleon's gone, Burger springs into action. He starts by darting over to the corner of the living room that makes up his bedroom and throwing a spare change of clothes into a bag.

Then he lifts his mattress and removes a vial of powder, still grateful the cops hadn't brought dogs. The habit had put him in a hole with people he wouldn't even want to caddie for.

It had gotten so bad that on more than occasion, he came home with a busted face and a lazily assembled story about some bar thugs that needed educating. Naturally, his friends had been concerned.

He always suspected Napoleon knew the truth. There wasn't much that escaped his notice, but for his part, he never said anything. After the third beating had cost him several teeth, however, he came home the next day to find a wad of money on his pillow wrapped in a rubber band.

There had been no note.

It wasn't enough to clear his debts by any means, but it kept the "creditors" off his back for a month and prompted him to decide then and there that he was going to get clean and pay back every penny he owed to his creditors and Napoleon.

As of today, he's still ten grand in the red with the interest mounting.

This last line had been intended as a reward for squaring his account. But now that an actual threat of death was in the picture.

When the last of it is gone, he grabs his bag and races for the exit, taking a second to stop as he passes the now open door to the bathroom. The sight of Skylar lying there is still so clear in his brain.

"We're going to get this prick, Sky," he says. "I promise."

Several blocks away, the hitman is watching Burger from the monitor in his hatchback. In the time between killing the girl and interrogating the witness, he had managed to set up some state-of-the-art spyware in their apartment.

Not wanting to be seen as he tended to the new wound in his shoulder, he'd moved to a nearby alley. Luckily, the bullet had passed straight through his shoulder and out the other side.

Yippie.

Unluckily, he'd been hit in the same shoulder where Milo had stabbed him, and it was fast becoming useless. He'd briefly debated calling it quits and writing this job off as a failure.

But pride was at the wheel now, and it didn't have a learner's permit.

He simply wouldn't accept the fact he'd been bested by two nobodies and his own gun. Granted, he had stolen the gun from someone else, so it wasn't technically his per se. But the point's still sound in principle.

And it meant war.

As he watches the blonde giant deliver his little speech to the dead before walking out the apartment and locking the front door behind him, he says to himself:

"Weird, I was thinking exactly the same thing."

Chapter 10

Napoleon adjusts the lapel of his white, tuxedo jacket as he sits in the back of the limousine. Having overlooked the fact that he'd need to change for the gala, he had done so with the limo's partition as his only source of privacy.

The process caused the cut on his cheekbone to reopen. He'd initially considered not addressing it because the thought of everyone at the gala being shocked and confused by him made him laugh.

Then his practical side took over, and he had Wescott stop for a first-aid kit. He realized it'd draw too much attention and likely inhibit him from being to skulk about and gather clues effectively.

Like I don't know who it is already.

All signs so far pointed to Adalyn Eadwulf as the prime suspect in Milo's murder. For starters, she hadn't seemed at all torn up by his death. She also knew where Napoleon lived, despite him never telling her his address, and her invite to lunch had coincided perfectly with the hitman's break-in.

But the cherry on the top of this fucked situation was that she'd been willing to throw him off the scent by hiring him to focus his attention elsewhere—at the other members of her family. Presumably, the plan was to keep him close while the hitman searched for the flash drive.

Bright lights are reflecting off his sleeves from the starry night sky feature on the limo's ceiling and wall trimmings. It would almost be pleasant if he wasn't seething with anger.

Not wanting to clue Wescott in on how he is doing for fear of the observation being relayed, Napoleon buries his emotion as he looks up through the partition and asks, "What do you think, Wescott?"

"Superb fit, sir," Wescott says, glancing in the rear-view mirror.

"It is, isn't it? Especially since I never told Adalyn my height and weight. I wonder how she knew my measurements so well."

"Miss Eadwulf was able to infer simply by looking at you, sir. She's had thorough schooling in an array of trades and disciplines, two of which happen to be design and ergonomics."

"Detail-oriented, is she?"

"It's a necessity in her profession." Wescott turns back to the road. "I understand that's something you and she have in common, sir."

This guy's been briefed on how to answer my questions.

"What is her profession, if you don't mind me asking?"

"She's on the board of directors for E Technologies."

"Never heard of it."

"That's not surprising. It's not a particularly alluring industry. They mostly deal in the manufacturing and distribution of compounds for the preservation of agricultural interests."

Napoleon raises an eyebrow. "Pesticides?"

The car phone resting on the shelf to the right of his seat starts ringing.

"That'll be for you, sir," Wescott says.

Napoleon doesn't answer right away. He's never had a phone call with a murderer before. Part of him is relieved.

Right now, he isn't sure how he'll react to seeing her in person. This feels like a good way to gauge things.

"This isn't a telemarketer, is it?" he asks, doing his best to mask the poison in his voice as he picks up the phone.

"Why is it that whenever I put men in tuxedos, they all start talking like they're international spies?"

Her voice is equal parts sultry and jovial. The situation apparently calls for amicability betwixt employer and employee.

Napoleon almost laughs; they were meeting at a fundraiser for bees, and she was trying to catch more flies with honey.

"You do this often?" he asks, going along with the banter.

"Wescott tells me you look like you've been in a fight."

"And here I thought we were building a rapport."

"Care to explain what happened?"

"I was attacked," he says, being deliberately curt. "I think it was the man who killed Milo."

"Any idea why he might have targeted you?"

You know why.

"He seemed to be under the impression I had a flash drive of some kind."

Adalyn doesn't respond right away. Napoleon even double-checks the line's still active before she comes back with: "I take it you don't?"

"Sorry to disappoint. Sounds like you know about it though."

"I have a few obligations I have to attend to. Once you've arrived, make your way over to the bar. I'll send someone to retrieve you when I've finished."

"You're the boss."

"And Napoleon?"

"Still here."

"If you see your former boss tonight, I'd advise walking the other way."

"Wha—" The line cuts out before he can finish asking his question.

As he sets the phone back on its receiver, he feels the limousine begin to slow down.

"We're here, sir."

Napoleon steps out of the fancy cab to find himself on the corner of 230th and 5th street. He notes several stragglers in black ties and gowns idling outside the building directly in front of him. A glance up at the rooftop reveals strobe lights shining out across the skyline.

"An ivory tower in the concrete jungle," he mutters as he walks inside.

He is greeted by a security checkpoint made up of an armed detail, several metal detectors, and a ticket taker of significant stature.

"Ticket, sir?" the ticket taker asks with all the charm of a ball trimmer.

"Ticket?"

"This is a private event; a ticket will be required to enter."

"Of course." He nervously begins patting down the pockets of his tux. "Let me just—"

A quick search reveals there's an envelope in the pocket of his jacket. Ironically, it's marked with a winking smiley face. Upon inspecting its contents, he discovers a ticket to the venue as well as $5,000.

They hadn't discussed when he'd receive compensation, and rightly or wrongly, Napoleon had assumed it would be when he finished the job. Yet, Adalyn had just given him half up front.

Why? Was it guilt?

He hands over the ticket, it's scanned, and he's permitted to pass through the metal detector. As he ascends to the roof, an overwhelming sensation of grief pours over him.

The walls feel like they're closing in around him. Adalyn is screwing with his head. Why bother paying him? Why not just fire him after a couple of days under some bullshit pretense? She couldn't feel guilty, could she?

He's not an expert, but he imagines anyone capable of killing blood isn't subject to such qualms. A shudder travels down his spine as another thought comes into his mind.

Is this fun for her?!

The elevator doors open, and Napoleon beelines for the bar, his eyes peeled for any sign of Adalyn or Cindy in the crowd.

Despite his hatred for Adalyn, it's difficult to disagree that bumping into his former boss would likely lead to a chat that he isn't particularly interested in having right now.

The bartender perks up as he nears.

"I'll have a be—" His voice trails off as he spots the "Open Bar" sign propped up on the counter several feet away. "Whisky. Neat."

"Any particular kind of whisky?" the bartender asks.

"Give me one that pairs well with aggravation and tragedy."

I may have a drinking problem.

"Aggravation and tragedy." Someone chuckles to his right. "That's good. I've never heard that one before."

Napoleon turns and just about falls off his bar stool. There, sitting at the end of the bar, very much alive, is Milo.

***

Ballistics managed to tie the Colt 1911 discovered at the scene of Skylar Lewis's death to the gun used in the killing of Milo Eadwulf. The assailant had evidently filed off its serial number to complicate efforts in sourcing its origins.

As luck would have it, forensics technology was improving every day. They had managed to pull a reconstructed image of its numeric sequence using microscopic imaging off its base-level engravings.

It is registered to an address in Queens and had been reported stolen several days prior to Milo's death.

Its owner is a woman in her late seventies. She'd acquired the firearm to give her a measure of home security but hadn't owned it for more than a week before it went missing.

At first, she thought she'd simply misplaced it. An easy story to believe considering the Coke-bottle glasses that Cayden could see she's wearing.

But after combing over every inch of her home and finding no trace of it, she realized it'd been stolen.

"Would you mind showing us where you kept the gun, ma'am?" Cayden asks.

"Of course, do come in." She moves out of the way to let them cross the threshold. "Please excuse the mess, I wasn't expecting company."

No truer words have been spoken. It becomes immediately obvious to both Cayden and Douglas upon entering that Irene's eyesight isn't her only sense that's going.

The old lady's townhouse can best be described as a hoarder's wet dream with the lovely scent of cat piss.

"Christ above," Douglas whispers. "There's morgues that smell better than this place."

"Shaddup," Cayden says, offering the old lady his best fake smile as he tries not to breathe through his nose.

"You know, there's a pattern developing of you trying to silence me that I don't quite—"

"Whereabouts should we be looking, ma'am?" Cayden asks in between coughs.

"What was that?"

Oh my god, she's deaf too.

"I said whereabouts did you keep the gun, ma'am?!"

"There's no need to shout, I keep the gun right here." She sets her hand down on a stack of newspapers sequestered behind an armchair in front of the bay window. "That way, I could get to it quick if someone broke in."

Both detectives' shoulders slump as they simultaneously realize that any two-bit criminal walking past could've easily spotted the gun from the street.

Useful prints will be unlikely thanks to the cat lounging atop its surface. And the collection of junk covering every available surface in the place pretty much guarantees that finding leads will be nothing short of a headache.

They'd just hit a dead end.

"Smart, wasn't it?" the old lady asks.

Cayden sighs. "Very."

Chapter 11

"You all right, friend? You look like you've seen a ghost."

Focus. Milo is dead. You're not crazy. This isn't his ghost.

Sure enough, as the panic subsides, pieces begin falling into place. Adalyn had said that every member of her family would be at this event. A brother would certainly qualify.

And this was definitely Milo's brother. They look too similar in age to have been father and son. There are also no bruises on his face and no bullet holes in his chest.

Their style, however, is a different matter and one of the main reasons why Napoleon hadn't really believed his sanity was slipping.

While Milo had been wearing a more casual ensemble, this brother is wearing a pitch-black suit from jacket to tie, as if in mourning. His hair's also more disheveled than Milo's had been.

Noticing this makes Napoleon relax a little.

His rationale being that if he had actually cracked and was now seeing "the dead", then surely, they'd be wearing what they'd worn when they'd died. Ghosts didn't change their clothes, that would be preposterous.

"I'll do a whisky too," says the brother to the bartender.

"You got it."

Napoleon relaxes further. Still, to avoid staring, he decides to divert his gaze to the venue around them.

There's an air of legitimacy to this ploy as having stepped out the elevator with tunnel vision and the singular goal of getting a drink as fast as possible, he hadn't bothered to stop and assess his surroundings.

The place looks great.

Lights run the outer rim of the ledge, serving to both illuminate the area and prevent people from falling off the side. A rented stage has been assembled over the top of the built-in brick bar, giving everyone on the roof the ability to watch the band.

This strikes him as an act of considerable foresight given that what space isn't occupied by standing-room tables is being claimed by guests.

What he appreciates the most, however, is that his attempt to distract himself appears to be working. Although his head is still thumping somewhat, his hands are no longer trembling.

He chooses to celebrate this revelation with whisky.

"You're the guy who saved Milo's life," says the brother.

Napoleon chokes and coughs as he spits out his drink. It suddenly occurs to him that this meeting is much too convenient to be a coincidence.

Questions swirl around his mind on a current of alcohol: Why hadn't Adalyn told him Milo was a twin? Why was the twin here now? Were they working together?

"I wouldn't say that," Napoleon says, having realized he'd let the brother's comment hang in the air far longer than was appropriate.

"Why?" he asks. "Because he died anyway?"

"I mean—"

"You stopped to help. That's more than most people would do. And you gave Polli a chance to say goodbye."

Polli.

Napoleon recalls Adalyn mentioning the name on the phone to Wescott while they were at the hospital.

"Milo's wife," the brother says. "Father never approved of their marriage, but that's not saying very much." He takes a drink. "There's little that passes for acceptable with him, the miserable turd."

Napoleon's not sure how to respond. The silence doesn't linger long, however, as upon setting his glass down, the brother extends his hand out toward him.

"Name's Kaleb."

"Napoleon."

They shake hands. It's at this point, Napoleon notices that Kaleb's knuckles are sporting a semi-yellow, semi-purple tint.

"Tell me something, Napoleon," he says as he picks up his glass. "Why does my sister think you're hiding something from us?"

"I wasn't aware that she did."

"I wouldn't be talking to you if she didn't." He signals the bartender for two more whiskies. "So what is it? He confess his affinity for reality TV in his final moments?"

"What makes you sure she's even right?"

Kaleb shrugs. "She usually is. It's why she's number two in the company despite being the youngest out of the three of us. Her natural business acumen pretty much guaranteed she'd take over when father stepped down."

"I have to say," Napoleon finishes his drink, "I didn't know him that well, but from what I gathered, I would've thought your brother was the genius."

"Oh, he is. Was. One of those whatchamacallits. Prodigies. He was solving equations at ten that father tackled as thesis questions for his doctorate." He smiles. "Never cared much for the people side of business though. Which worked out well because Adalyn wouldn't be caught dead in a lab."

"So if your brother inherited the engineering prowess, and your sister, the business mind, what does that make you?"

Kaleb smiles as the bartender sets another two whiskies down in front of them. "Every family has a black sheep."

As he takes a drink, Polli approaches.

"Look who it is," says Kaleb.

"I've been sent to fetch you both," she says sullenly.

She's wearing a dark-green, slim-fitting dress that starts just off the shoulder and seems to draw Napoleon's gaze to her cleavage.

Not wanting to stare, he opts for direct and heavy eye contact, prompting him to notice that her makeup has smeared.

"Hello, Napoleon."

"Polli . . . I was sorry to learn about your husband. I know what it's like to lose someone you care about."

"It sucks."

"Yeah."

She stares off into the middle distance and sighs before continuing, "I wasn't aware you knew Adalyn."

"We met earlier today at the uh . . . hospital."

"And she just invited you to this out of the blue? You think that being here is appropriate seeing as how he's dead now?"

Napoleon pauses. "She told me her family wanted to meet me."

"Ha!" Kaleb laughs. "Typical over-achieving Adalyn, the one time she brings a guy home he's literally a life-saver."

"No, he isn't," she says sternly.

Her tone prompts Kaleb to raise his hands in mock surrender.

"Well, you'll forgive me if I avoid you," she says, her glare shifting to Napoleon. "I came here tonight to avoid wallowing in misery and right now you're just bringing up a lot of . . . sadness."

"I understand."

And Napoleon did understand. God knows, when he sees Adalyn all he'll be thinking about is Skylar.

"Don't worry, hero," Kaleb says, "I'll hang out with you. I could use a drinking buddy."

"No, you couldn't," Polli says. "And you're not staying here, Kaleb. All three of us have been summoned backstage."

"I love it when you talk to me like that," Kaleb says impishly. "It's so authoritative."

Polli reacts by taking his drink out of his hand and swallowing it in one gulp. Before Napoleon can react, she does the same with his too.

"Come on," she says as she turns and storms off into the crowd. "The keynote's about to start."

***

It had taken one cab ride, two detours, three unnecessary metro changes, and a partridge in a fucking pear tree for Burger to finally shake the itch at the back of his neck.

The sensation might just have been cocaine psychosis, but there was also the possibility it was well-founded paranoia. Regardless of credibility, he had managed to arrive at his destination without incident.

Having recently changed ownership, the nightclub is currently closed for renovations. Its prior proprietors had been forced to sell after the place had been shot up by some nutjob too disenchanted with life to cling to anything even remotely resembling a moral compass anymore.

That'd been the official story anyway. But Burger knew the truth. The club had caught the eye of some very bad men. So they had made a non-negotiable offer to take the headache of running the business off the owners' plate.

It had been refused.

With darkness falling on the street, the sliver of light peeking out from behind the tarp covering the club's front window is extremely noticeable.

It's the only place Burger could think to go. For one thing, he knows they'll have guns, which, given that he is potentially being hunted by a professional hitman, would be useful. Also, despite their dislike for him, he knows they'll protect him because of the money he still owes.

That wouldn't be forgotten simply because he's now on the run.

Third, and he can't overstate the importance of this part, is they might take pity on him and share a line or two. Or ten. Or even just one. He steps out into the street at the mere thought, completely neglecting to look both ways.

Luckily, no cars are coming. In fact, if not for the one guy selling fireworks, and the other limping toward Burger, the street would be deserted.

"Wait," Burger says to himself as he squints, suddenly recognizing the shaved head. "Oh shit!"

Chapter 12

Napoleon and Kaleb follow after Polli as she leads them across the roof, past a wall of security, and back behind the stage at the top of the venue.

Several yards away, Napoleon sees Adalyn conversing with a man who looks old enough to have given the first instructional lectures on how to make a fire.

Seeing that they've arrived, Adalyn gestures for him and the rest of his present company to idle nearby until she and the old man have finished talking.

The impulse to eavesdrop overwhelms Napoleon.

He notes a snack stand on the adjacent side of a curtain near where she and the old man are standing. It's separated by a slew of security guards and personal assistants who, like him, are awaiting instructions. Presumably, it's for production staff, but he can't imagine anybody would say anything about him getting a bag of chips.

He offers to get Kaleb and Polli something as well but they both decline.

The guards ignore him for the most part, but Napoleon decides not to press his luck by dragging his feet.

As he reaches the snack stand, he's relieved to know that he'd been right to assume he would be able to hear what Adalyn and the old man are saying:

"That covers everything," she says. "You all set?"

"I've changed my mind. I'm not going out there."

She sighs. "We've been over this already."

"I'm disgusted by the sight of these hypocritical leeches."

"Most of the people out there have been your friends for decades."

"What do I say?" he asks rhetorically. "Hmm? What have I always said? In this tax bracket, there are only colleagues and people you don't have leverage over yet."

"Yes, I believe I've seen this particular rerun," she says mockingly. "Any chance we might be able to switch channels?"

The old man scowls. "Don't be sardonic. It's so common among women your age it borders on a literary trope."

"Oh, and the contemptuous billionaire is an original persona? Look, if you aren't seen to be unaffected by this campaign being circulated in the press, you'll be approaching competitors from a position of weakness."

"So all of sudden you're supportive of the sale? Do forgive me for not realizing, I've only our last few dozen conversations to use as data."

"Okay, well now who's being sardonic?!" She pauses to gather herself together. "If you want to sell, you have to be willing to play ball here."

"Don't talk to me about how to play ball," he says, adjusting his suit jacket. "I taught you how to play ball."

"Does that mean you're going out there?" she asks.

He doesn't answer. Napoleon tries to adjust his position so that he's able to see through the curtain as well as hear them and accidentally kicks the base of a roadie's black tour case in the process.

When neither of them reacts to the sound, he's overcome with a palpable sense of relief comparable only to that feeling of taking a mint from the host stand at a restaurant and them not saying anything about it.

"Mom would've wanted you to," Adalyn says.

The old man raises a stern finger toward her. "Watch it."

From his vantage point, Napoleon watches as the old man shifts from anger into a dispirited sigh. He pinches the bridge of his nose before turning to address the group of assistants nearby. "Who has my speech?"

One of them hurries over with a packet of flashcards.

"You're a great white in an ocean of elephant seals, Adalyn," he says as he slips the cards into his jacket.

"Someone's been googling animal food chains."

"Don't be ridiculous. I have people to do that for me."

The old man walks out on stage to thunderous applause as Napoleon slowly sneaks off in the opposite direction. He opts to bring a bag of chips with him, thinking it'll help cultivate an air of legitimacy to his alibi. He notes a hint of discomfort on Kaleb's and Polli's faces at his sudden return that gives him pause.

"Can I get one of those?" Kaleb asks, gesturing to the chips.

"I just offered . . . Fine."

Napoleon hands Kaleb the bag of chips as Polli's phone rings. "Yes? . . . We're on our way." She hangs up before turning to address them both. "Showtime."

***

"Who's found you?"

Yash leans against the bar on his slender arms, his eyes fixed on Burger through thick sunglasses.

Samar, Yash's business partner, has been put on edge by the sudden intrusion and Burger's not-so-subtle display of fear as he stands in the open doorway to the dance hall like the ugly girl at prom.

Nestor, on the other hand, seems unbothered by it all. His focus is currently being held by the comically large pre-roll he's got between his fingers as he lies sprawled out on a couch in the VIP section.

Yash knows this ease has more to do with Nestor's general approach to life than the semi-automatic residing on the coffee table just within his reach. Despite being more of a partaker than partner most days, he was a helluva shot. And could be damned scary when he wasn't sitting on his ass.

That said, renovating the club was proving to be a slow, irksome progress, and the fault lied with them all. The other two had suggested hiring a crew to handle it but they hadn't at Yash's insistence.

He thought it would be a good idea to take a break from the more adrenaline-inducing parts of the job and focus on something a little less stressful. In retrospect, it wasn't the smartest decision he'd ever made.

"I need a gun," Burger says more brazenly than perhaps he should have. "Would someone please just give me a gun?!"

"I'll give you a gun all right," Samar says, picking up a shotgun and aiming at him.

"Woah! Woah!" Burger raises his hands out in front of him as if it would do any good before reflexively taking two steps back, falling, and hitting the ground tailbone-first.

"Hey, hang on," Yash says, moving next to Samar, who's now looming over Burger. "Let's everybody just chill out for a second. Samar, how's about we put the gun down?"

"Like hell," Samar says. "Who's looking for you?"

"A hitman, all right?!" Burger shouts. "He might be special ops, possibly a ninja. I don't know, but he's killed one of my friends already and now I'm pretty sure he's hunting me!"

"And you led him here?!" Samar's eyes dart around as Nestor coughs up smoke from the corner of the dance hall. "Not cool, man."

"Look, I needed a place to hide and—"

"So, you thought here?!" Samar runs over to the window to peek out behind the tarp.

"I think you might be overlooking an important detail here, partner," Yash says, clasping his hands together. "We have a client in our place of business who has need of our services. Urgent need. The kind of need that would benefit greatly from access to our . . . premium package."

Samar raises an eyebrow. "Premium package?"

"The likes of which include security personnel, a personal firearm, and an all-expenses-paid stay in the finest defensive stronghold New York City has to offer."

Samar smiles maliciously. "Oh, right." His attention returns to the window. "The premium package."

"Seriously?" Burger asks. "You're raking me over the coals now?"

"That's capitalism, baby." Yash cleans his glasses with his shirt. "She be a cruel, opportunistic bitch, with one hell of a checkered past."

"Fine," Burger sits upright. "How much?"

"Twenty grand."

"Are you high?!"

"Very!" Nestor pipes up from the back of the room.

"I don't have that."

"We're willing to lend credit at interest." Yash makes it sound like he's doing Burger a favor. "But that means if we kill this guy, you owe us twenty on top of the ten already, deal?"

Burger could cry. He doesn't want to say yes, but it feels like he has very little choice. The hitman was here. Frankly, he's surprised he hadn't shown up already.

"Deal," he says, softly.

"Great!" Yash tosses him an AMT Hardballer before then grabbing his fully automatic and throwing the strap over his shoulder. "Then let's kill a ninja."

As if on cue, the lights cut out, and the room goes dark.

"You had one job, Nestor," Yash says, irritably. "How could you forget to pay the electric bill?"

"Uh . . . I didn't."

"Guys?"

"What is it, Samar?"

"Am I the only one who hears fireworks outside?"

Before they can pull back the tarp to see if any fireworks are actually going off in the street, Samar's shotgun fires.

In the split-second flash that follows, Burger can make out the silhouette of a man decked out in covert ops gear as he pulls Samar off his feet, over his shoulder, and onto his stomach. Seconds later, the darkness returns, and the sound of a bone snapping is followed shortly after by Samar's screams of anguish.

Then all hell breaks loose.

Yash lets it rain through the dark in the direction Samar had fallen. Nestor quickly follows his lead.

To avoid getting caught in the crossfire, Burger opts to stay low to the ground with his head covered. Gunfire lightens up the room enough every few seconds for him to catch his bearings.

Having spotted a door to the kitchen at the far end of the hall, he urgently begins crawling toward it. There's another round of gunfire, and then everything stops.

So he stops. Several seconds pass before he hears the dealers reloading.

"Did we get him?" Nestor asks.

"Shhh, I don't know," Yash whispers.

"Should we ask?"

Before Yash can respond, Nestor's neck is snapped from behind, triggering more gunfire that urges Burger forward.

As he makes it to the kitchen door, he allows himself one last look over his shoulder just in time to see the silhouette of a man dive behind the bar seconds before it's lit up with what is more than likely the last of Yash's ammunition.

Fear takes over as Burger pushes through into the well-lit kitchen and begins searching for an exit. He quickly locates a door and runs in its direction, only to find that not even putting a shoulder into it will get it to open.

"No," he whispers. "No, come on."

Once. Twice. The third try dislocates his shoulder. It's as if it's being blocked from the other side.

Is this really it? Is this how it ends? How long can he keep this up? He can't evade this guy all night. And say he catches him? He gets the flash drive too. Then there's nothing to stop him from getting away.

But if he gets rid of it? If he hides it somewhere the hitman would never think to look. Napoleon can still make things right; justice can still be served.

For both of us.

The decision is made. For the first time in his life, it feels like a real decision. Even if he doesn't win today, he can take solace in knowing the hitman is going to lose.

Probably. More than likely.

Enough with the doubt already!

He starts by sending a text. It's followed by another quick scan of the kitchen, this time, in search of a hiding place. The place is massive and looks to be occupied by a never-ending number of potential options. But he's after something specific: a place that only Napoleon would think to look when he inevitably tracks him to this address.

After several precious seconds of searching, he finds it.

A sudden absence of the sound of gunfire suggests he doesn't have much time left.

He quickly hides the flash drive before deleting the text he sent as he moves to the center of the kitchen with the AMT in his other hand, fully prepared to go head-to-head with a man responsible for five deaths in two days.

Surprisingly, despite having already fought him once, not to mention the hundreds of hours he'd logged playing video games, Burger feels somewhat unprepared.

With a shaky hand, he cocks the trigger as the sound of approaching footsteps invites him to reflect on his life.

He fires at the kitchen door.

BLAM! He hadn't been ambitious, never had what some might consider a vocational calling.

BLAM! BLAM! But he always tried to do right by those who mattered to him. He can't help but laugh.

The second this notion enters his head, it's immediately followed up by the realization that had he not just lent Napoleon some cash when he'd asked—

BLAM! BLAM! BLAM! He empties the chamber. Everything is quiet for some time after that.

When the footsteps return, James is forced to confront the harsh reality that his KD ratio is about to change forever. He drops the empty gun and picks up a frying pan off a nearby stove. If nothing else, he's going to go down fighting.

"I'm coming, Skylar," he whispers. "I'll see you soon."

As the hitman steps through the door, he charges forward, wielding the cooking utensil over his head like a mad man.

"Blackjack motherfucker!"

Chapter 13

"Thank you for coming, everyone."

Having reached the podium at the center of the stage, the old man straightens his back and looks out at the crowd.

A quick internet search identifies him as billionaire Stanton Eadwulf. Recent articles do nothing to paint him in a positive light. However, a lot of the gripes seem to focus more on his lucidity than his social class. There are numerous references to his alcoholism, aging, and professional competency. Most of it looks like it's sprouted within the last six months.

They'd begun shortly after the death of his late wife, Lillian. She'd supposedly been spearheading several sustainability efforts in a part of the world Napoleon isn't that familiar with when she'd fallen ill.

But more surprising to him is that most of the articles have been written by none other than his former boss, Cindy Li.

Her angle is pretty much the same as the outliers, if not more critical. Professionally speaking, they strike him more as flat tabloid hearsay than her typical high-quality work.

He looks up from his phone as the crowd applauds Mr. Eadwulf's latest remark.

Napoleon finds it rather gross that the head of a pesticide manufacturing company can speak so passionately about preserving the Earth, considering that anyone with a basic grasp of biology knows that pesticides are bad for bees.

So for this professional bee butcherer to get up on stage at a fundraiser dedicated to their preservation and wax lyrically about their vital role in mankind's continual cohabitation with the planet speaks volumes.

Also, the man has no stage presence.

His closing comments acknowledge the efforts of his brilliant daughter, Adalyn, in putting this gala together before ending with a call-to-action, encouraging everyone to dance, drink, and donate. He walks off stage to another round of applause that Napoleon doesn't think he earned.

"Amazing speech, Stanton," Polli says, taking his hands in her own. "You were so articulate."

"Thank you, my dear, I understand all too well how these last few days must have felt for you." He squeezes her hands in turn. "I applaud your strength."

She nods, teary-eyed, as his focus shifts to Napoleon. "And who might you be?" he asks.

"This is Napoleon Davis," Adalyn answers for him. "The man who helped Milo."

"I see. Will Mr. Davis be attending the memorial service at the house tomorrow?" Stanton asks.

"Tomorrow?" Kaleb looks at Adalyn. "Really?"

"It makes sense to do it while everyone's still in town."

"It would be my privilege, sir," Napoleon says, addressing Stanton.

He has no interest in spending any more time with these people than is absolutely necessary. But if he's going to find answers, he needs to work his own angles, not just Adalyn's.

And visiting their house would likely prove informative.

Napoleon does his best to avoid the daggers Adalyn's staring at him as he shakes Stanton's hand. Then Stanton's attention shifts from him to Kaleb.

"Son," Stanton says, offering out his hand.

Kaleb accepts it. "Satan—I mean, Stanton."

"How's sobriety going?"

"About as well as it is for you, I hear."

Damn.

"All right," Adalyn says. "Let's go mingle."

"I think, perhaps not," Stanton says.

"We had a deal, dad."

"Fine, half an hour."

Polli leads Stanton out into the crowd as Kaleb picks between his teeth and says, "Well, it looks as though my boyish charm and devil-may-care attitude are no longer required. And since my cup appears to have runneth empty, I shall bid you all a dewy."

"It's adieu, isn't it?" Napoleon asks.

"Gesundheit." Kaleb grins, burps, and strolls away.

"Come dance with me," Adalyn says, taking Napoleon by the arm. Her voice now carrying a guise of sensuality that he can't help distrust and feel enamored by at the same time.

They walk through a horde of some of the wealthiest men and women in the world until they emerge on the dance floor. As if on cue, the band changes their playing from an up-tempo swing to a more tranquil piano ballad.

Given that he now knows Adalyn put this event together, Napoleon wonders how many of the evening's events had been arranged before the night even started. And to what end?

She pulls him close, resting her head against his torso as they dance. It infuriates him to be so near to his friend's killer, but he can't bring himself to pull away. He needs to stay on her good side, at least for the time being.

Why ask him to dance though? What is she after? Has the hitman found Burger? Does she know he has the flash drive? He received a text from him while googling information about Stanton but had gotten caught up in the introductions before remembering to open it.

He slows his breathing. It's all he can think to do to prevent himself from pushing Adalyn away and frantically pulling out his phone to check his messages. She smells so good.

You're an awful human being.

"You look nice," he says, pushing this thought from his head.

She doesn't answer.

The band's song nears the crescendo. Its soft, melancholic tonality appears to be putting the dancers around them in a harmonious, trance-like state. There's an eerie beauty to it that says a lot about the intrinsic socio-economic nature—

"You're fired."

"I'm sorry, I didn't quite catch that," he says, taking this in.

"I hired you to find out who in my family killed Milo." She's still leaning on his chest. "Not to eavesdrop on my father and me."

"A good journalist looks at things from every angle."

"Your loyalty's been called into question. I don't hire people I can't trust."

"I'm guessing Milo was untrustworthy then." His response comes instinctively, his words, full of malice. She takes her head off his chest to look him in the eyes.

"Was that why you had him killed?" he asks. "Was his loyalty called into question?"

"Come anywhere near the memorial service tomorrow, and you'll wake up on a beach hundreds of miles from a US embassy without so much as a pocket dictionary."

The song crescendos as they separate before coming to a halt. The room's atmosphere has shifted from a calm lull to a rigid tension and it's soon followed by the distinct sounds of a man shouting, a hand hitting flesh, and a woman crying out.

Prior whispers and muffled talk warp into horrified gasps. Napoleon can just make out Cindy hurriedly heading for the stairs in the opposite direction of a red-faced Stanton.

Stanton is being encouraged by Polli to take deep, calming breaths as their security detail begins to form a protective circle around them.

"You can keep the tux," Adalyn says. Her parting words.

Deciding he'll probably have better luck asking Cindy what happened than an Eadwulf, Napoleon starts pushing through the crowd towards the stairs.

Upon reaching them, he glances down over the banister in time to see his former boss reach a level several floors below, shoes in hand, and disappear through a door. He sighs.

Terrific.

Realizing he won't be able to catch up to her before she's gone, he turns his attention to Burger's text. It consists of a drop pin to an unfamiliar address and a single misspelled sentence:

"gid im forus, napo"

It takes him a second to decipher what it means. When he does, his heart drops. Frantically, he calls a cab.

***

It would be three years.

Three years!

One surprise visit to his work, and they'd all been flushed down the toilet. Which was a fitting metaphor, since she had found him fucking some skanky goth-looking bitch in a handicap stall at the bar he tended.

He'd followed her out onto the street in a final, desperate attempt to convince her that he'd made a mistake, but she'd had none of it. Tears were shed, threats were hurled, and the onlookers were many.

The scene eventually culminated in Maggie's declaration that she was moving out, and Tommy was instructed to stay away from their apartment that night so that she could pack without having to look at his stupid face.

He'd agreed without objection, which, for some reason, hurt her more than all the rest of it. In a blind rage, she had smashed his forty-inch plasma with a hammer as she left.

"I mean, I tried to tell you that guy was a douche rocket," Grace says as she and Maggie sit side-by-side in her apartment, passing a joint back and forth.

"No, you didn't. You told me you thought he was really sweet and kind actually."

"I did?"

"Yes!"

"Hmm . . . must've been high."

"Yeah, well. From here on out, I'm no longer dating nice guys. Give me an asshole any day of the week. At least then I'll never be surprised."

"Sounds healthy."

"I mean, why in a bathroom?" Maggie leans forward and puts her head in her hands. "Of all the places he could've . . . Could they not smell it in there?"

"Were they standing?"

"What?"

"Like was she straddling him on the toilet seat? Were they up against the wall? Or were they doing it Aldo style?"

"You're a pervert."

Grace coughs up smoke as she laughs.

"Honestly," Maggie says, trying not to laugh herself. "What difference does it make how they were doing it?"

"Well, if they were standing up, there's a chance her bare ass was rubbing up against the nasty wall, getting all sorts of bacteria on it."

"Is that supposed to make me feel better?"

"Only if it happened."

Maggie puts another chunk of ice cream on her spoon; she's eating it straight out of the container.

"They were doing it Aldo style."

"Ah, shame."

Aldo, Grace's red and brown Leonberger, is rolling around on the floor in front of them. Maggie loves Aldo.

He never barks, barely ever whines, and it's easy to tell when he is happy because he smiles like a moron.

"It's all my fault, isn't it?" Maggie asks, almost crying.

"Yep."

"Dude."

"What? You're funny, your boobs are enormous, and you can pretend to care about baseball. I'm surprised he didn't cheat on you sooner."

"Thanks for having my back. How's that law degree coming along, by the way?"

"I switched to the culinary school; snacking's less frowned upon." Grace sets what's left of the joint down in the ashtray. "Speaking of which." She gets up from the couch. "Wanna know what goes great with ice cream?"

"A bottle of wine?"

"What are you? A soccer mom? No, mushrooms. We're about to trip hairy balls."

"Christ."

Chapter 14

Soot, shreds of paper, and firework residue coat the street in front of the nightclub. The door is open, but none of the lights are on either inside or out. It's quiet.

Napoleon's despair grows as the door creaks open, and the carnage of the dance hall comes into view. Blood covers the walls and furnishings, and bricks of cocaine are scattered on the floor. Every step he takes kicks empty gun shells in all directions.

In one corner, the bullet-ridden corpse of a man he doesn't know lies in a contorted mass on the floor. It's so dark that he doesn't even see the second body until he trips over it.

After he's regained his footing and his eyes have adjusted to his surroundings, he realizes that he's standing next to the bullet-ridden remains of a third man propped up on a stool like a dollhouse reject.

It's then that he notices the industrial light hanging off its hinges as it flickers through a window panel on a door at the back of the club.

Instincts forged from years of watching horror movies are screaming at him to run the other way, to leave this sweat-inducing nightmare behind, and never return.

But he's already lost one friend that week. Two would simply be unacceptable. He falls to his knees.

Two would be unacceptable. Two is unacceptable. No.

He tears up. "Nooo."

James is lying on an aluminum table in the center of the kitchen. His internal organs are hanging over the sides of the large hole where his stomach used to be. The knife the hitman had threatened Napoleon with is on the table next to him.

Napoleon vomits. It's too much. He can't understand it. Can't bring himself to look at his friend. Naively, after what happened to Skylar, he didn't think his heart could break any further.

Break.

He wants to break something. Doesn't matter what, so long as it's expensive. But a glance at his surroundings reveals most of the area has been upended already.

Hang on. Why? The thought suddenly occurs to him.

If James had been tortured for information, presumably the whereabouts of the flash drive, why bother searching the kitchen?

Napoleon forces himself to study his friend's corpse. Something's missing, but it takes another few seconds for him to realize what: there's no rope. James isn't tied to the table. If he'd been tortured, surely he would have had to have been restrained to prevent any resistance.

But he isn't, so he wasn't?

To get a full 360° view, he takes a lap around the table. A large chunk of the back of James's head is missing. There's also a hole under his chin.

It's crushing to see, but it's enough to confirm that unless the hitman removed his bindings after he died, which seems unlikely, James was dead before he was cut open.

It would be a lie to say knowing this made Napoleon feel better, but at least James hadn't suffered. Physically.

He shudders to even imagine the fear he must've felt in the lead-up to it. Not wanting to dwell on these thoughts any longer, he decides to act.

James's innards had been searched because the hitman hadn't found the flash drive on him. The kitchen had then been searched because the hitman hadn't found it in him.

What did that mean?

For one thing, James didn't have it on him when he died. But that didn't mean the hitman had found it in the kitchen.

Napoleon starts with all the areas left untouched by the destruction: a shelf of boxes filled with dinner plates, the cabinets under the wash station, and the inner wall of vents hanging over the top of the stoves.

Finding nothing, he turns to the mess. The more he looks, the less he finds. And, in turn, the more stressed he becomes.

If it isn't there, he'll be without a magnet, and his friends will have died for nothing. The thought alone is too much to bear. He doubles his efforts.

Just as he's on the verge of having exhausted his options, he notices something out of the corner of his eye. Peeking up from under a litany of cooking pots and refrigerated produce several feet away is an overturned mini fridge not unlike the one in their apartment.

Every inch of both it and its contents are then meticulously scoured until, at long last, he finds it hiding in a packet of string cheese on a shelf in the door.

After a celebratory first pump, he collects himself to decide his next move. A theory is brewing in his head as to how the hitman knew James had it but testing it will involve taking evidence from a crime scene.

He briefly debates if he should just wash his hands of the whole situation, share everything he knows with the authorities, and simply walk away.

But he can't. That much he knows. Instead, he gets to work on formulating a plan.

Step one involves hightailing it out of this place. When he's far enough away, he'll send an anonymous tip to the police about possible gunfire from this location. He can't afford them getting in his way right—

His phone rings. He answers in a blind fury. "Yeah?!"

"Napoleon, you unreliable fuck! Where the hell are you? Your shift started half an hour ago! I got a wedding reception here packing the place tighter than a duck's asshole and nobody running out the artichoke and spinach crostini!"

"Sal?"

"Wha—Course it's fucking, Sal! Why aren't you at work?!"

It's at this moment that Napoleon realizes he forgot to get someone to cover his shift at the catering company.

"Yeah, I can't even begin to tell you how much that isn't a priority right now."

"Is that right? Well, try this on for size, jerkoff. You're fired!"

"Oh, no." He hangs up and goes back to developing a plan. By the time he reaches the front door of the nightclub, he knows what he's going to do.

"Freeze!"

He freezes. Having walked back out onto the soot-laden street, he finds himself staring down the drawn weapons of three squad cars' worth of law enforcement as a TV crew documents the scene from a safe distance.

Evidently, someone had beaten him to the phone.

Chapter 15

"Six murders in two days. You going for a world record?"

Douglas is leaning against the wall, his arms crossed as he studies the suspect with a combination of smugness and disdain.

Napoleon hadn't said a word their entire way back to the station and was presently refusing to even look up from the metal cuffs that locked him to the aluminum table.

"That's fine," he says, pushing himself up off the wall. "You don't have to say anything. We've got you placed in the alley where the body of Milo Eadwulf, son of billionaires Stanton and Lillian Eadwulf, was discovered earlier this week." His tone is light. "A case currently being ruled as a homicide. We've got you placed in the apartment where the gun used to shoot Milo Eadwulf was found along with the body of Skylar Lewis, a known associate of yours. Her death, which, at one point, was being ruled as an accident, has since been upgraded to homicide thanks to the colorful statement you provided."

He sits down in the chair opposite Napoleon as he adds, "*And* we've got you placed at a nightclub where not two, not three, but *four* bodies were discovered. One of which, also used to belong to a known associate of yours!" He laughs. "To top it all off, you cut him open and rifled through his intestines, thereby adding a mutilation of a corpse charge to an already impressive murder resume." He leans forward on the table. "Got a couple of questions about that last one, by the way. You mind filling me in on some of the details?"

Neither a flinch nor gesture is picked up by the several cameras studying Napoleon's every move. His tuxedo jacket has been confiscated because of the bloodstains it acquired after he had tripped in the club. With it are the flash drive, his ticket to the gala, and the envelope of money Adalyn had given him. After documenting his belongings, they'd taken his prints, and left him to fester.

"Five grand's a lot of cash to be walking around with," Douglas says. "Some people would kill to have that kind of money."

Napoleon just stares at the ink and blood on his hands.

"What about the knife you used? A custom make with a poison compartment built into the handle? That's a pretty impressive feat of engineering for someone with no engineering background. Where'd you get it?"

There's the faintest glimpse of an eye roll.

"You'd be saving me a lot of paperwork if you just confessed now, you know?" Douglas says, trying to mask his irritation.

Silence.

"I need a cup of coffee." Douglas rises to his feet. "You want one? Black, I take it?"

Napoleon's nose crinkles slightly.

"No?" With a shrug of his shoulders, Douglas walks out.

On the other side of the reflective glass window separating the interrogation room from its observation deck, Cayden stands scratching his chin. They're getting nowhere, and, to him, it's obvious why. He doesn't even bother to turn around as Douglas walks in. "Perp's a brick wall." He hits the brew button on the side of the coffee maker. "I doubt he'd sing if the fat lady herself conducted his tempo."

"Any luck with the flash drive?" Cayden asks.

"None. They've been at it for hours. It seems the whole thing's coded to fry itself if the third password attempt is incorrect, so they're doing nothing until we give them a stronger lead."

Cayden struggles to control his coughing. "How many attempts do we have left?"

"Two. Who cares though? We've got the murderer."

"You think so?" He almost laughs.

"I do," Douglas says, pouring a cup of coffee before pointing at the glass. "That's our guy."

"His clothes are way too clean to have been anywhere near that gunfight. None of his prints are on any of the guns we found, and there's no powder on his hands."

"So he wiped his prints and covered his suit. Why are you overthinking this? We can place him at each location."

"He called them in!" Cayden tosses the gala ticket on the table. "He's got alibis for all three murders."

"Then why run?! Why'd he hitch a ride to the hospital after Eadwulf was found?"

"You know why." He coughs again. "You spoke to the EMT."

"No, I know what the EMT *said* happened, but I don't know if it's true. Davis could've paid her to say all that shit about a lapse in judgment and forgetting protocol."

"Or it could've just been plain old medical negligence."

Hill sets his coffee down.

"Look, Junior, I know you've been a detective for all of what, three minutes now? And I get it. You're eager to solve your first big-boy case, so let me help you out. We found *one* of several murder weapons in his place. He knew *two* of the victims personally. And he is carrying *three* times more—"

"Have you read the street vendor's statement?" Cayden asks, his frustration mounting. "The one selling fireworks? His description of the guy setting them off in the road perfectly matches to the one Davis' and Miller gave us of the killer."

Douglas shakes his head. "You can't trust that. The poor guy was panicking about taking a rap for illegal contraband. Our boys could've been leading his answers for all we know."

"What about the blood under her fingernails? Or the blood on the shards of glass?"

"Same theory as the EMT. He could've strangled Lewis, paid Miller to corroborate his story and planted blood under her fingernails to throw us off the scent."

Cayden's eye twitches. "Do you hear yourself?!"

Before Douglas can respond, the door opens, and a woman in her late sixties walks in as if she owns the place.

Both of them immediately stop arguing as she meanders over to the glass panel to observe the suspect handcuffed on the other side. Her own hands clasped behind her back.

"Lieutenant." Cayden clears his throat. "How can we help you?"

"This him then?" she asks.

"Sure is, boss," Douglas says.

"Well, he's definitely a suspect, but we're not 100 percent certain yet that—"

"Call's just come in from Washington. Seems the federal fellas think one of the guys on their naughty list is in New York, and they have asked for the details on the Eadwulf killing."

"How did they—"

"What did you tell them?" Cayden asks through a fit of coughing.

She raises an eyebrow. It's directed at Cayden.

"It's the dust," he explains. "Nothing contagious."

"I told them the truth, Detective. I told them we've got a high-profile homicide open that, for some miraculous reason, still hasn't hit the press. As well as several low-tier drug killings that are *supposedly* connected."

Coughing fit having subsided, Cayden just looks irked now. While Douglas, who's far more experienced with these sorts of interferences, just falls into a chair and kicks his feet up on the table. He already knows where this conversation is headed.

Contract killings were FBI's jurisdiction, which meant they'd soon be on their way to take control of the investigation. He and Cayden had just been relegated to the sidelines.

"Look, they get here in the morning," the lieutenant says.

Everything from the men's button-down to the furrowed brow permanently ingrained in her forehead spoke to her many years working the job.

"As of an hour ago," she adds. "You're to hold off on pursuing any leads in this investigation—"

"Ma'am, with all due—"

"And all evidence turned over to the Federal Bureau of Investigations! This is happening, Freeman. Act like a professional."

Seconds after she's gone, Cayden kicks a chair and sends it barreling into the wall on the other side of the room.

Douglas finishes his coffee. "Don't remember temper tantrums being in the handbook."

"You're not funny."

"Oh well," he sighs as he chucks his empty coffee cup into the trash. "No sense us hanging around if we don't get credit." He heads for the door. "I'm gonna go ahead and pull seniority and leave you to tidy up. I've got a six pack of beer waiting for me at home and to be honest, it's about time I deleted the voicemail, know what I mean?"

"No, but I don't want you to explain it either."

"And what you want, you get, right? Just so we're clear, *partner*, if you ever try to silence me again, I'll let the lieutenant know how not contagious that cough really is."

Cayden raises an eyebrow.

"You know what I mean," Douglas says, realizing he hadn't come off quite as threatening as he'd intended. "Just . . . respect your elders. Fuck!" He storms out.

All things considered, going home sounded pretty good to Cayden. But he'd never been one to tolerate unanswered questions. It's what had given him his edge as a cop and helped him rise to the rank of detective so quickly.

Still, ignoring direct orders was, historically, not known to have ended well. So, if he's going to follow through on what he's thinking, it will require some serious discretion. At least, until after he can drop the bad guys at the proverbial feet of the powers that be.

The fact of that matter is he was a good detective and felt no need to apologize for that fact. A lot of men's ambitions drive them to chase power and satiate greed.

For Cayden, it would only ever mean catching criminals.

If that also meant playing fast and loose with the rules—as the saying goes—then what the fuck. It was a means to an end.

He hits brew on the coffee maker, quickly downs a cup, before crumpling up its remains and tossing them into the recycling can.

***

Energized by several awful but very necessary caffeinated drinks, the sleep-deprived hitman is air drumming away on his steering wheel to an equally awful but necessary metal song. To say he was exhausted would've been an understatement considering the bags under his eyes.

He's parked in the alley several blocks from the witness's apartment, staring at a live feed of the living room, which is streaming from spyware in the apartment's air vents to the portable monitor on his dashboard.

There are also tags on both Davis's passport and driver's license, so he'll be alerted if he tries to skip town. Not that Davis could afford a plane ticket. Or a bus pass for that matter.

In fact, it was his abundant lack of resources that had the hitman thoroughly convinced he'd eventually return.

It's just a matter of waiting.

His burner rings. He sends the call straight to voicemail. There's nothing to report to her right now.

Chapter 16

"What aren't you telling us?" Cayden asks, sitting down in the chair across from Napoleon.

True to form, Napoleon doesn't react.

"Maybe that's too vague a question." Cayden strokes his chin. "Why'd you lie to us about having the flash drive?"

Again, nothing.

"All right, how about we start with its password?"

Napoleon stirs at this revelation. "What password?"

"Come on."

"It's encrypted?"

Cayden furrows his brow. "As far as we can tell, we've got two attempts left before the whole thing craps out on us and whatever's on it gets deleted forever."

He studies Napoleon for any tells suggesting that he knew that already. None are apparent, and he'd already switched off the tape in the observation room, so watching the footage back would be out of the question. It wasn't his smartest play, but he couldn't afford a record of the breach in protocol.

"Why did you lie to us about—"

"I didn't lie," Napoleon cuts him off. "I found it after you left."

"You didn't think to reach out to us?"

Napoleon ponders the question. "No."

"Why?"

"I don't know." He sighs. "Time constraints?"

"Time constraints? How busy are you that you can't pick up a phone and dial three numbers?"

There's a pause.

"I want to catch this guy."

"Because he killed your friend?"

"Friends," Napoleon meets Cayden's eye. "Plural."

Cayden nods. "So you figured as long as you had what he was after, you were gonna cross paths again?"

When he doesn't respond, Cayden clicks his tongue. "I don't like vigilantes. They preach impartial justice, but I've always found their rationales aligned more with vendettas than altruism."

"I'm not a vigilante."

"You ain't a cop neither." Cayden leans forward. "And regardless of how many people you've lost, you don't get to cowboy up without due process."

That's rich, coming from me, Cayden thinks.

Napoleon looks back down at the table. If the conversation is to continue, evidently Cayden will have to do a lot of the heavy lifting.

"Any idea what's on it?" Cayden asks.

"No."

Cayden deflates.

Before he can make up his mind as to whether to press him further, Napoleon perks up. A realization falls over his face that quickly changes to a knowing smile. "But I might know its password."

"What is it?" Cayden's eagerness is evident.

Napoleon pauses. It dawns on him for the first time since this nightmare began, he has something in the realm of leverage.

"You seem like a good guy," he says after several seconds have passed.

"Thanks, that means a lot."

"But you keep racist company, and I don't know how much of what you've been saying is truly reflective of your character. Your partner's made it pretty clear I'm looking at some rather colossal accusations going forward, and right now, the only bargaining power I have is keeping you from the whole picture."

"You said you might know the password."

"So make me a conditional offer." Napoleon opens out his hands in a display of friendliness. "You guys do that all the time, right? If I'm correct, and the code is what I think it is . . ."

Cayden racks the table with his knuckles as he mulls over his response. He'd anticipated their talk going this way from the start and had been prepared to make a deal from the moment he entered the room.

Still, there was no sense in disclosing that without seeing how much of the puzzle Davis would willingly give away first.

"I'll drop three out of the six homicide charges and the corpse mutilation," Cayden says.

"Full immunity from prosecution, in writing, and a forty-eight-hour window without police interference."

"Fuck you."

"In exchange," Napoleon continues, "for the password, the hitman responsible for all six murders, and the person who hired him."

"You can get all that in forty-eight hours?"

He shrugs. "If I can't, our deal is nullified, and I go before a judge. How's that sound?"

"You'd take your chances with a public defender?" Cayden smiles before adding, "If I close the file right now, you'd go down, you know? And I'd likely get a promotion. Maybe a medal."

"Maybe. That is until the real killer comes looking for the flash drive, which I'm guessing he will, seeing as he was willing to kill four people tonight just to try and get it back."

Cayden coughs again.

"Look, I'm not saying you couldn't frame me." There's a tinge of sorrow to Napoleon's voice now. "Discredit my alibis, bury evidence, fabricate a motive. I don't doubt I'd get life. Crazier things have happened. So if that's the route you want to go, then fine."

Shit, he's got survivor's guilt.

"I just need to ask one question."

"And what would that be?"

"How long did they give you?"

"What?"

"The doctors. How long do you have?"

"How do you—"

"Your cough," Napoleon says solemnly. "It's not a cold or one of those forty-eight-hour cases of flu. Otherwise, you'd have taken time off to recuperate."

"It's asthma."

Napoleon shakes his head. "It's not asthma. You would have used an inhaler. And it isn't that you're one of those weirdos who's obsessed with working all the time. Though that was my initial guess. You are young enough after all that your position as a detective could suggest that you're either a savant or singularly focused."

Cayden looks stunned, so Napoleon keeps going, "But you're in shape. You exercise regularly. And it isn't vanity motivated, or, no offense, you'd be bigger and a lot more outspoken. I'd wager it's about maintaining a balanced lifestyle—work hard, play hard, and all that." He shifts in his chair. "It also explains why your partner puts up with you taking the lead on things, even though he's got years of experience on you. It's pity. He knows you won't be around long."

Cayden stifles a cough as he crosses his arms.

"You're dying, detective. And while you aren't married to the job, you are using it to distract yourself from that reality."

"What's with the envelope of cash?"

"Adalyn Eadwulf paid me to try and figure out who killed her brother. How long have you got?"

"We're not talking about me. Why'd she hire you?"

"Apparently, I'm unassuming. And I had a good reason to be around her family since I'm the one who found him."

"She thinks someone in her family killed him?"

"I'm not a liberty to discuss ongoing investigations, but, yes that's correct. Anything else?"

Cayden smirks, taps his index finger against his forearm, and sighs. "Six months. They gave me six months."

Holy shit, he's actually dying? I should take up Texas Hold'em.

"What are you doing here, man?" Napoleon asks. "Why aren't you on a beach somewhere drinking Mai Tais?"

"I don't like sand . . . Full immunity, a twelve-hour window."

"Twenty-four."

"Ten. And you have to deliver on all three; code, killer, and contractor. Deal?"

"Deal."

"Alive, by the way."

"I figured."

"I mean it." Cayden's face grows serious. "Your friends are dead. You're in the clutches of grief. And you have survivor's guilt."

"You're a therapist now?"

"I'm a cop. One that's going against my better judgment and breaking all sorts of rules because, frankly, I don't think you killed anyone. But that doesn't mean you're not capable of murder."

"Then why let me go? Seriously, your partner clearly thinks I'm guilty. So why are you so willing to cut a deal?"

Cayden does nothing for several seconds before shrugging. "Crazier things have happened, right?"

Napoleon looks skeptical. "Right . . ."

"All right then, what's the password?"

"Fuck you." He smiles. "You'll get a password when I see something in writing."

Cayden sighs. "Was worth a shot."

He moves to stand from his chair but stops as a Hispanic man with a briefcase barges in through the door, panting heavily.

"Sorry, I'm late," the man wheezes. "It took me forever to find parking, and the lady at the front desk was on the phone with her friend for twenty minutes talking about some guy she thinks might be the father of her child, but she wasn't sure because she'd taken the bus recently and—"

"Time out," Cayden says. "Who are you?"

"Dante Hernandez." He straightens his tie. "Public defender here on behalf of my client, Napoleon Davis, who's invoked his right to remain silent, so you've no business—"

"Hey," Napoleon says. "Hey, it's all right. We're all good here."

"What's that now?"

"Yeah, Davis and I have just finished cutting a deal."

"Cutting a deal?"

"It's true," Napoleon says. "So thanks, but your services won't be required."

Dante looks flabbergasted. "You—Are you sure?"

"I mean, you're welcome to stay and read through the contract just to make sure this guy—" he gestures to Cayden—"hasn't tried to sneak in anything that we haven't discussed."

"Don't give me any ideas now," Cayden says, half-joking.

He and Napoleon both laugh. Though Cayden's quickly devolves into a coughing fit.

"Apart from that," Napoleon says, regaining his composure. "I don't think there's that much left to work out."

"Uh . . . okay." Dante's not sure what to do with himself. "Anybody need anything from the break room?"

"Ooh, I wouldn't say no to a carton of orange juice," Cayden says. "Davis?"

"Nothing for me, thanks."

"Orange juice . . . Right."

As he leaves, Cayden turns back to Napoleon. "I'll be right back with the paperwork. I've just gotta make a call first."

"I'll be here."

***

Hill's doing ten over the speed limit as he races home with his police siren on. Another few minutes, and he'd be sitting on his couch with a beer in one hand and the TV remote in the other, perhaps with the leftover pizza from the fridge on his stomach.

His phone rings. Seeing it's Freeman, he groans. They'd been alright at first. Had even taken a weekend trip to Florida with his friends to drink and gamble. But he'd been such a stickler for the rules and "due process" that it made him insufferable.

Although, there had been a noticeable shift in his approach lately. It started with little things like neglecting paperwork or letting perps off with warnings when there should've been arrests. He grew more introverted and insubordinate, and while some of it might've just been the job wearing him down as it was known to do, it didn't explain his work ethic. He'd develop these insane fixations on cold cases, some of which were twenty years old.

And then there was the coughing.

Tailing Freeman to his doctor's appointments had been too easy. Besides, he'd evidently had a lot on his mind.

Cancer.

Direct confrontation had prompted Freeman to reveal his diagnosis as terminal. He had less than a year.

Freeman pleaded with him to keep quiet about it, not wanting to be declared unfit for duty and forced to spend his last few months sitting around, waiting for the end. And because he's such a nice guy, Hill had agreed.

And because Freeman had conceded to Hill's word being the last word, they'd take on everything they worked up until he croaked.

But recent arguments suggested that Freeman was starting to forget that proviso.

Fine by Hill; he's tired of working with him anyways.

Freeman had dared to silence him in front of witnesses like he was his superior or something. It makes him seethe just thinking about it.

His phone rings again. The urge to send it to voicemail is strong, but he knows it'll just keep ringing the more he tries to avoid it. He lets it play a few more seconds before answering.

Chapter 17

"Sign here, here, and here."

Having reviewed and approved the pages of the contract with Napoleon, Dante's motioning to various signature boxes that he needs to sign. On the other side of the glass, Douglas stands perturbed, while Cayden, who's standing beside him, noisily works his way through a cup of orange juice. *Obnoxiously* noisily. Like a vacuum or in-laws.

"This is such bullshit," Douglas grunts.

"Relax, if he can't deliver everything within the ten-hour time frame that we've allotted him, then the whole deal is nullified, and you still have your prime suspect."

"How do we know the flash drive is even relevant, genius? He's the one who told us about it in the first place!"

"It's relevant." He takes another sip of orange juice.

"I'm taking this to the chief. Along with everything else, I hope you realize that."

"You do that, and I'll share those photos of you and that drag queen in Miami with the entire bullpen."

Douglas goes pale.

"My personal favorite is the one where you're sitting side stage and she's taking the money out of your hands with—"

"All right, all right!" Douglas gestures for him to stop. "Fuck man, I thought you said you didn't care about shit like that?"

"Me? I don't." He smiles. "But you do."

"Hang on a second, if you had pics from that night, why'd you not just threaten to share them when I found out about your—"

"Because it's much easier to be mean after you've been nice than it is to be nice after you've been mean."

There's a pause.

"What?!"

When Cayden doesn't elaborate further, Douglas, now very pale, turns back toward the glass to see Hernandez flipping through the contract one last time before placing a copy in his briefcase, shaking Napoleon's hand, and walking out the interrogation room.

At which point, Napoleon spins round to face the reflective glass. "Hey fellas, how many fingers am I holding up?" He gives them the bird.

Eyes follow the trio as they stroll past the bullpen toward the forensics lab. An uncuffed perp being escorted, not led, in the opposite direction of holding is, evidently, an odd sight to behold. So much so, that one cop feels obligated to ask Douglas what's going on as he passes by.

Douglas, sporting a notable aura of dejection, simply sighs and mumbles something about how the whole world's gone crazy.

There's only one technician in the forensics lab when they enter, a Hindi woman in her thirties, wearing a tattered lab coat that's hanging loosely over a set of gym clothes. Her hair is tied in a disheveled knot at the top of her head as she leans against a sterile white counter, drinking a cup of tea. She looks tired.

"Hi, Hermal," Cayden smiles. "You know if Bill's around? Some evidence got brought into him earlier, and we—"

"He's taking a smoke break." She pushes a set of green-tinted glasses up the ridge of her nose. "If you're wanting to open that drive though, I can help you out with that."

Napoleon's heart just about sinks into his colon.

"You what?" Cayden coughs.

"You're able to hack into it?" Douglas adds, a hint of optimism to his voice.

"No, its firewall is too intricate. And from what I can gather, its system operates off a rotating catalog of coding sequences programmed to position themselves at the substructural base of the software in a nonsequential order every half an hour."

Hermal didn't enjoy making people feel stupid. She's just good at it. It had been an issue she'd come up against her entire life.

The intricacies of her brain made so much sense to her that it was easy to forget that not everyone shared her doctorate in computer engineering. Or psychology.

Or the biology of arthropods.

As the familiar painting of dumbfounded faces appears before her once again, she sets her cup of tea down and proceeds to make shapes with her hands as she says, "Imagine the lock to your house changing every half an hour based on a dice roll."

"Okay," Cayden says, skeptical. "So how do you plan on opening it?"

"I've been working on a computer algorithm that automates the process of character profiling." She turns a nearby monitor toward them to reveal the program running on her screen. "With the Eadwulfs being public figures and everything, I was able to input a vast library of data on events in Milo's life that could've potentially left lasting impressions on his psyche." She ambles back to the counter to get her tea. "When correlated against his writing style, which the algorithm can quantify thanks to his years publishing research, it's able to generate the hundred most likely options, accounting for numerical values, capitalization, and special characters."

Fuck.

"Looks like we won't be needing you after all." Douglas sneers at Napoleon. "How long till we get that list?"

"About . . ." Hermal glances at the monitor. "Thirty seconds."

"And will the list be organized by likelihood?" Cayden asks.

"No, I wrote the code to sort based on astrology sign."

PING! The computer signals that the program has finished calibrating, and the four of them gather around the monitor. There before them is a list of a hundred potential password options, which are allegedly organized by order of likelihood and science.

Two elements immediately stick out to Napoleon. The first is that the top ten options on the list are entirely comprised of capitalized letters. The second is that the code he had been planning to try didn't seem to be anywhere on it. And he can't tell if that makes him feel better or worse.

"Bailey?" Cayden asks. "What's Bailey?"

Hermal, who, before, had been the physical embodiment of hubris, now looks sheepish, borderline embarrassed.

"It's . . . his mother's maiden name."

Everyone pauses for a moment.

"That some kind of joke?" Cayden asks.

"Well, she did die six months ago! It wouldn't be a huge leap!"

"I say we try it," Douglas pipes up. "At least the first option. If it doesn't work, we've got one guess left, and suspect number one here gets a shot at saving his bacon."

"Fine." Cayden coughs. "Where's the flash drive?"

Hermal retrieves it from a nearby workstation and plugs it into the side of the desktop. She double clicks on the mouse to pull up a landing page with one interactable text box.

The code is entered.

A palpable sense of relief floods over Napoleon when it doesn't work. It fades quickly, however, as it occurs to him that just because their guess was wrong doesn't mean his will be right.

If he's anything remotely like the private investigator he'd been pretending to be over the last few days, now would be about the time for a speech or, at the very least, an internal monologue about how right and wrong were often so close and yet so far away.

But he isn't even walking in the rain with a cigarette hanging out of his mouth, so what's the point?

"Son of a bitch!" Douglas shouts as he kicks a nearby table. "Try the second choice."

"No," Cayden says. "It's Napoleon's turn."

Both he and Hermal move out of the way so Napoleon can approach the keyboard. His legs feel like they're going to give out from under him. Freedom is on the line now. He'd made a promise he wasn't sure he could keep, so naturally, life had come to test his metal.

Stupid life.

He starts typing.

Chapter 18

"Cocksucker?" Hermal asks as Napoleon hits the enter key. "Why would it be cocksucker?"

"Does it matter?"

"You don't actually know, do you?"

"Doesn't matter."

"Look!" Cayden points at the monitor.

They all watch as a buffering dial appears. Seconds later, the landing page is replaced by rows of folders labeled with specific dates. The singular exception to this organizational system is a folder entitled, "Plan Bee". It had worked.

It had actually worked.

Napoleon can't contain his excitement. "Let's go!" he shouts, starting the other three.

"Jesus Christ!"

"Sorry."

"Why would you do that?"

"Who the hell is this guy, Cayden?" Hermal asks.

"Too complicated to explain right now. So we've got it open, now can we find out what's on it?"

Hermal nudges Napoleon out of the way to take over the keyboard. She starts with "Plan Bee", presumably because it's the only folder without a date. That, and for whatever reason, it's been highlighted green.

She clicks on it, and it opens to reveal an assortment of documents, blueprints, and video logs.

"The hell is it?" Douglas asks.

"It looks like a design for an artificial bee," Hermal says.

"Okay," Cayden says. "Why would Milo be carrying around a design for an artificial bee?"

Napoleon smirks.

"What?"

"It's a flash drive," he chuckles. "A universal serial bus?"

None of them have a clue what he's suggesting. This only makes it funnier.

"Otherwise known as a USB." He smiles. "Or, in this case, a US*Bee*. Get it? Cause of the . . . I'm allergic."

Groans, disheartened sighs, and threats of being arrested again follow as Hermal clicks on the latest video log.

What plays is a recording of a mechanical bee flying over and landing on the anther of a tomato plant. It lingers there briefly before rising into the air once more, only to then land on the stigma of a different tomato plant across the lab.

"It's . . . pollinating," Hermal says. "He must've been trying to develop an artificial substitute to combat the extinction of bees."

"Try?" Cayden asks. "It looks like he succeeded."

Hermal frowns as if having this opinion is idiotic. "There are over twenty thousand different species of bees on the planet and they're all designed to cater to different kinds of plants. To create a substitute that could handle all different types of pollination would be . . ." She trails off.

Instead of powering down as she'd anticipated, the artificial bee is now moving toward a blueberry plant. Her jaw drops as she watches it repeat the pollination process it just completed several seconds earlier, but now for a completely different species of plant.

"That's . . . not possible."

"Could it be CGI?" Cayden asks.

"I don't know what it could be," Hermal says, exercising some patience. "I do know it isn't a sustainable alternative for the natural process of pollinating."

"Are you sure?"

She's surprised by Napoleon's question. "Absolutely."

"Because a lot of people have died for someone to get this back. Doesn't that suggest it could be worth something?"

"I'm not saying it isn't worth something. I'm *saying* there's no way it can sustainably replace thousands of years of an evolutionary infrastructure without a catch."

"But it—"

"Oh, for God's sake!" She turns back to the monitor.

"What are you doing?" Cayden asks.

"Quiet."

As they wait for her to finish whatever it is she's typing, the three men sit idly in a feeling that's not dissimilar to the awkward tension of a clinic waiting room.

"Here we go," she says after several minutes. "I've just run the folders through a script searching for variations on the word *complication*, *unintentional*, and *drawback*."

"Neat."

"For these things to be capable of meeting the physical demands of their programming, it looks as though they need to be capable of autonomously, anatomically, restructuring themselves."

"Is that difficult?" Napoleon asks.

"From what I can gather, Milo's solution to this problem centered around creating a synthetic compound that could accommodate the various biological makeups of individual bees for the particular plants they're pollinating."

"So he figured it out?"

Hermal glances at him irritably before continuing to read, "The manufacturing process of this compound is such that were it to be produced on a large scale, we, as a species, would be dealing with an ecological fallout that'd rapidly accelerate beyond existing scientific predictions.

"What the hell does any of that mean?!" Douglas asks.

"It *means* that the process of making these bees will do more harm to the planet than they'll solve." She turns to Napoleon. "You convinced now?"

"I am," he smiles. "You've been a big help."

She's taken back.

"When did my ten hours start Cayden?" he adds.

"When you signed the dotted line."

"Sounds like I need to get going."

***

The hitman chases down his burger with an aspirin and a swill of soda. He hadn't accounted for a stakeout on this job and had been forced to grab something quick to stay near Davis's apartment.

Sitting around doing nothing is causing all the adrenaline of the last few days to wear off, and he's starting to feel the weight of his injuries, of which there are several.

If nothing else came of the next few hours, he knew one thing for certain; his cheeseburger had a hair in it.

The portable monitor signals there's been motion detected. A glance at it reveals Napoleon Davis, the witness, entering his apartment, taking off his tuxedo jacket, and setting an envelope down on the table.

He starts the ignition and throws the hatchback into drive. The commute won't take long, but he can't afford to lose him again. The longer he's in New York, the more he can feel the noose tightening. Things had gotten complicated so fast, and all because this guy had felt like sticking his nose where it didn't belong.

He decides he'll use his hands to kill him. No strangulation, no body shots, just a good old-fashioned bashed-in skull.

The sound of a shower running pulls his focus back toward the monitor in time to catch a glimpse of Napoleon tossing the flash drive up into the air, catching it, and then sliding it into his pocket as he walks into the bathroom off the kitchen, shutting the door behind him.

The hitman smiles.

Chapter 19

For three people that lived in New York, they had all failed to grasp the importance of simple security measures.

Had Skylar Lewis locked the front door after James Miller had gone to work, things might've gone differently. Had Miller been smart enough to not corner himself off, who's to say he wouldn't have gotten away? And Davis, the witness.

The fact that he'd dropped out of college suddenly makes a lot of sense to the hitman. He seemed incapable of learning, whether from books or the mistakes of others.

The hitman tries the handle as he approaches the door and slides the lock picks back into his pocket. Once again, they proved unnecessary.

Bummer.

Upon entering, he clocks the shower's still running before moving to inspect the envelope resting face down on the table. As he turns it over in his hands to see if any clues might shed some light on where Davis has been, confusion takes a meaty hold.

Something's off.

It has no address, no return address, and no stamp. All that's on it is the word *Boo* followed by a semi-colon and the right bracket of a parenthesis.

The realization comes too late. Before he has a chance to react, he's hit hard over the back of the head. His vision goes blurry, and his ears start to ring as he falls to the wooden floor.

He wakes to the smell of cigarette smoke. His head hurts, as do his wrists. He's been tied to a chair by some bondage ties; this does nothing to reassure him.

He makes note of the fireplace ablaze in the corner before the sound of the water switching off in the bathroom behind him makes him tense involuntarily.

Then Davis appears in his periphery.

He struggles against his restraints as Napoleon casually sits down in the chair across from him.

There'd been no consideration made for the blood flow in the hitman's hands. Not wanting to dwell on the implications of this decision, he turns his attention to making sense of what had just happened.

Davis is still in the tuxedo, which suggests that he never had any intention of showering. The running water must've been a diversion to lure him into thinking he had the upper hand, same with the open front door and envelope.

Now he realizes how Davis managed to get the drop on him.

It was partly the same reason he'd been forced to make his hasty exit out the window the last time he'd been there: the fire escape was only accessible from the bathroom.

Davis must've climbed out onto it and down to the street to wait for him to show up. He probably followed him up the stairs.

Sloppy.

"I'm two for two tonight, you know," Napoleon says, taking a drag of his cigarette. "And it looks like I was right about you bugging my apartment."

While the hitman's involuntary glance is subtle, it doesn't go unnoticed. Napoleon turns to see what he's looking at and his eyes fall over the air vent in the ceiling at the far corner of the living room. There's a knowing smile on his face as he turns back around to face the hitman.

"You're off your game a little bit, aren't you?" He gets up from his chair and walks over to the vent. "I mean, you're a pro. There's no denying that, but I suppose even pros have their limitations, right? Especially given everything you've been through the last few days."

Despite knowing it's futile, the hitman continues to wrestle against his bindings as Napoleon begins to unscrew the bolts to the air vent.

"A knife wound, two gunfights, and sifting through James' organs couldn't have been pleasant," he says, casually. "Plus, I mean, no offense, but you don't look great. Kind of clammy and . . . putrid."

As he removes the last of the screws in the ceiling vent, it drops down from the ceiling along with the spy camera hiding inside. It's roughly the size and shape of a shirt button.

Picking it up, Napoleon turns and holds it over his head in a gesture of celebration. Not surprisingly, the hitman doesn't share his enthusiasm.

Napoleon shrugs. "No one would hold it against you for not being at 100 percent." He walks back over and sits down. "How could they?"

When the hitman says nothing, he turns the spyware over in his hand and adds, "This thing's wirelessly transmitting to a receiver, right? Judging from how fast you showed up and the keys I found in your pocket, I'm guessing that it's in your car?

You wouldn't be willing to disclose if it's got playback capabilities, would you? Or if the footage is exportable? Where'd you park by the way?"

The hitman's semi panicked now. The way Davis is talking so casually to someone he must despise has him concerned. And right now, he's in no position to protect himself should Davis suddenly snap.

"That's all right," Napoleon says. "I'm sure I'll be able to figure it out." He stands up, walks over to the fireplace, and picks up a branding iron that's been heating in the flames. "I'm more interested in knowing who hired you."

Despite being farther away from the fire, the hitman's sweating profusely. The iron's shaped like a heart, which freaks him out almost as much as the fire.

And he does not like fire.

"I have my own theories obviously," Napoleon continues as he starts walking slowly toward him. "But that's all they are right now, are theories. So, if I could just get you to confirm a couple of details for me, it would really help justify a lot of the legwork I'm going to have to make up over the next . . ." He checks his watch. "Seven hours. My, how time does flitter away."

They were in the early hours of the morning but it was still dark, and Davis hadn't bothered to turn on any lights. This compounded with the luminance of the iron shining upwards on his face gave him a menacing aura so dramatic it bordered on theatrical.

When the hitman doesn't respond, Napoleon sighs.

"You know, I consider myself quite resilient, I mean, up until recently, I was working crazy long hours for crazy bad pay.

Whatever, I dropped out. If I have to do a bit more here and there to make up for that, so be it." His face grows serious as he starts rotating the branding iron in his hand. "But in the last two days," he adds, softly, "you have killed six people, two of whom were pretty much the only friends I had. And then you almost had me take the rap for it." The iron's held out toward the hitman's bare shoulder now. "A guy can only take so much in a single workweek, you follow me?"

Fear and the hitman have become one and the same.

"Who hired you?"

"I don't know."

"Bullshit."

"They made payments anonymously," he pleads as Napoleon moves the iron closer to his shoulder. "We only ever spoke through burners, but I'm . . . I'm pretty sure it's a woman!"

Napoleon pulls back. "What makes you say that?"

"She used a voice modulator." He can't hide his relief. "In my experience, only women do that."

"A bit sexist, isn't it? I feel like if I was hiring a killer, I would also want to prevent them from being able to recognize my—"

"It's not about disguising the voice. It's about authority. A deeper voice is more intimidating; it makes them more effective in negotiations."

There's a pause.

"A voice modulator, huh?" Napoleon pulls out his phone and sends a text. "Why the alley?"

The hitman hesitates.

"Why the alley?!"

"It was a last-minute switch. They—She called and said the target was leaving town ahead of schedule, and she wanted to move the job forward."

Another pause.

"Cool, well, I appreciate you helping out. There's a couple beers in the fridge and some leftovers if you're hungry. Other than that, I guess just sit tight. Police should be here shortly."

Napoleon drops the branding iron off at the fireplace before leaving, whistling as he goes.

Outside on the curb, he pushes the car alarm on the key he'd "borrowed" from the hitman until he finds a car parked half a block away.

As he drives away with the sun rising overhead, he sees two police cars pull up outside his building.

Two down, one and a half to go.

***

Maggie starts the morning by checking her phone; there are no texts or calls from Tommy. She hadn't wanted him to reach out. She just thought he would've.

As she sits on the couch, she notices that there's a glass of water, a packed bubbler, and a note from Dana on the coffee table. Her priority's the water.

They'd spent the night listing off all the ways that men were trash and hallucinating gigantic goldfish were swimming around the living room.

Naturally, this had taken a toll on her hydration.

As she drinks, she reads the note:

Gone to work. Hope you're feeling better this morning ☺ *. If you could let Aldo out when you get up, that'd be sexy.*

—D

Eerily, Aldo takes this moment to nudge her with his snout. Dana mentioned that he was prone to sleeping on the cold kitchen tiles because of his fur. But as the night had wound down and Dana had gone to find her bed, he'd plopped down on the carpet at the foot of the couch.

"Morning, handsome," she says, petting his head. "Mind if I hit this before we go out?"

He's a dog, so he doesn't respond.

Maggie stretches as weed meets her system before getting up to throw on a pair of flip flops and a hoodie. Sensing an outing, Aldo moves to sit by the door, where he stays until she puts on his leash.

The morning air is brisk as they walk out onto the street. Foot traffic's at a minimum.

Aldo does his business quickly, so she opts to take him around the block. Partly because she thinks he'd appreciate the exercise, but mainly because she knows all that's waiting for her back inside is a day spent crying, apartment hunting, and snacking. And crying.

One block quickly turns into two, and before long, she's trying to find a café for breakfast.

A glance at her phone's map tells her that there's one with outdoor seating not far away. Ideal for someone with a furry friend—the non-animal-costume-wearing kind at least.

A few onlookers and reporters are gathered outside a building flanked by a couple of police cruisers. As she approaches, she overhears snippets of a conversation between two people in pajamas, wherein the word "murder" is mentioned several times.

"What's going on?" she asks, pulling on Aldo's leash to get him to settle.

"Oh, just some psycho on a killing spree, returning to the scene of his crime."

"What?"

"Yeah, they think he murdered, like, a hundred people with a toothpick."

"Oh my God."

"I mean, that's twice now that this freak's broken in over the course of like two days. And nobody's done shit! Security here is freaking abysmal! What if it had been us?!"

"You can't start thinking like that, Anthony. You'll go insane."

"Last week I bought a $6,000 guitar, Christine. I am insane!"

Aldo's struggling to relax. All the commotion and flashing lights are putting him on edge. It takes several seconds of Maggie petting and cooing for him to even sit down.

Then the cops bring a man out of the building.

She doesn't recognize him right away. It's not until they make eye contact that the realization hits harder than the bubbler, and she almost lets go of Aldo's leash.

Aldo, for the first time in all the years she'd known him, is now barking, snarling, and snapping his teeth.

The guy from the restaurant?!

"I tell you something," Anthony says. "I'm renegotiating the terms of my lease. You can believe that."

Chapter 20

The elevator opens, and Cindy Li steps out onto the main floor of the Epoch Tribune. Nobody would be in for another few hours, but that worked for her.

She hadn't bothered to hide the bruise on her cheek. It'd likely spawn a couple of whispers and the odd comment from some of the bigger jackasses in advertising, but with any luck, it would also garner some sympathy sex come lunchtime.

She reaches into her purse for her office key as she nears the door but is surprised to find it's already ajar. A creature of habit, she knows she didn't leave it unlocked when she finished up the previous day.

Her concern quickly changes to anger, however, as upon pushing the door open further, she finds Napoleon asleep in her swivel chair. His shoes are propped up on her desk.

"What the hell are you doing here?!"

"Huh?" He sits up, suddenly awake. "Wuzzup?"

"You have ten seconds to explain before I call security!"

"What is it with everybody's natural inclination to count down from ten?" Napoleon yawns. "You ever think about that?"

"Start talking!"

"Ah!" He winces. "And here I was burning the midnight oil."

"You don't work here anymore, remember?" She crosses her arms. "You quit."

"You're right, I'm here for me." He gets up and strolls over to the window. "But I'm also here for Fawkes. I realized you probably hadn't found someone to replace me yet, which meant there'd be no one to water him today."

He picks up the bonsai tree, adding, "And I just wouldn't be able to live with myself if something happened to him. He and I are like two peas in a pod or . . . two plants in a pot, no that's not—"

"Give it a rest," Cindy says. "You and I both know it's fake."

"What? No, Fawkes is a fake? That's ironic for more reasons than one."

"The hell are you talking about?"

Lena the accountant suddenly appears in the doorway, out of breath.

"Lena?" Cindy looks surprised. "It's early for you to be here."

"What . . ." Lena says, breathing heavily. "What do you mean 'we have a problem'?"

"We have a problem?" Cindy's thoroughly confused. "I don't understand; I thought we had found a rhythm recently—"

"I'm talking about the email! Why did you message me saying we had a problem?"

"What are you talking about? I didn't—" Cindy trails off, her head swivels back to Napoleon.

He's still standing by the bonsai tree, his arms crossed as he leans against the wall. Only now, the phony surprise he'd previously been feigning has been replaced with a far more amused grin.

"You hacked my email?" She runs behind her desk to see if her computer has been unlocked.

"Hacked is a strong word. You don't even have a password. It's honestly a little ridiculous."

"Lena, call the police."

"Oh, I wouldn't do that if I were you."

"He's right," Cindy says. "I'll do it. Nothing would tickle me more."

"Okay," he says as she walks out into the hall. "I guess I'll just have to explain to them how you two are embezzling money from the paper!"

Lena's eyes go wide. A second later, Cindy reappears in the doorway, trying to keep her cool.

Napoleon smiles. "Hi."

"What do you think you know?" Cindy asks.

"You know what I never understood? How someone who *ought* to be making less than a hundred grand a year as a journalist—just based on statewide salary averages—affords penthouse real-estate on the upper east side?"

He starts pretending to browse the bookshelves on the wall. "I mean, you had me pick up a fur coat a few weeks ago. That alone has gotta be what, eight grand? Whatever, I didn't think much of it at first. After all, you could have family money, couldn't you?" He spins dramatically on his heels. "Then I began spending some time shifting boxes from one shelf to another in a nasty windowless storage room. Boxes made up of things like balance sheets, employment records, *expense* reports." He exhales like a horse. "I tell you what, it doesn't take long for boredom to take over in that situation. Sooner or later, you look for anything to do. Or read."

Lena gulps.

"Let me ask you something," he says as he stares directly at Cindy. "Did you used to buy all that stuff you had me pick up because you genuinely wanted it or because you got some sick, sadistic joy watching me race all over town like a friggin' pack mule?"

Cindy remains silent. Admitting the truth would do nothing but the fact of the matter was, she resented that he had been given an internship. He had minimal qualifications and little experience outside of several subpar articles he'd gotten published in his university paper.

His affiliation was disparaging to put it fancy-like.

"Well?" he asks.

"What do you want?"

"You've been publicly denouncing Stanton Eadwulf's mental stability since January. Why?"

She shrugs. "His wife died six months ago, and he fell off the wagon after forty years of sobriety. He's prone to outbursts, and now looking to sell a company that's done nothing but print money for his family since bootcut jeans were in."

"Last night you were at a gala where he gave a keynote."

"I . . . wait how—"

"While you were there, you two got into an altercation, right?"

"I wouldn't call it an altercation. He physically attacked me!"

"Were you paid to instigate a confrontation with him?"

Cindy feigns disbelief. "How *dare* you suggest that I would deliberately go out of my way to—"

"Were you?"

"Yes!"

"What?" Lena asks, turning to Cindy.

"By Adalyn Eadwulf?" Napoleon presses.

It's her turn to gulp nervously. He was coloring Lena's perception of her.

"By his daughter, Adalyn Eadwulf?"

"Yes, dammit, by his daughter!"

"How could you?" Lena takes several steps back from her. "You know what I've . . . What happened to . . ." She trails off.

"She offered you an exclusive, didn't she?" Napoleon asks. She told you that if you wrote some articles framing Stanton as insane to provoke him publicly, then you'd get the chance to break a story about the exciting new product they're preparing to launch that will *revolutionize* the future or something to that effect."

Cindy sighs. "She used the word *alter*."

"I can't believe this." Lena stumbles back against the wall.

"Sweetheart, please." Cindy reaches for her hand. "Please just give me a chance to—"

"Don't touch me!" Lena pushes her hand away. "Just . . ."

Cindy watches her leave. In truth, she can't blame her.

While Lena was in college, she got involved with someone who ended up being a colossal piece of shit. Her friends would regularly try to convince her to seek help but to no avail. Until, one day . . . avail.

She tried the on-campus help center, campus security, and the local authorities. The only notable reaction her story provoked was in the man. And it wasn't a positive one.

Eventually, things got so bad that Lena had to transfer.

She didn't date for a long time after that. It wasn't until after she graduated and moved to New York that she even felt ready to try. Then she met Cindy.

Cindy, who Lena just learned had taken the emotionally scarring experience that she'd shared during pillow talk and had used it as strategic fodder to further her career.

Cindy had hoped that with the right framing, Lena would come to see it the way she did. That, in a lot of ways, what she had done to Eadwulf was a victory for all women, including her.

But the chances of her seeing it like that now were ruined. Thanks to Napoleon. As furious as she is with him, she can't help but be slightly impressed.

"Fake plants, fake errands, fake journalist." He lifts a finger with every entry he lists off as he passes her on his way out of her office. "It's ironic!"

"I trust this means I've earned your silence?!" she asks as he walks down the hall and steps on the elevator. "Napoleon?"

The elevator doors shut.

Chapter 21

"Ah shit."

Back in the hatchback, Napoleon's looking at the arrival time the routing software has estimated for the drive to the Hampton mansion. It's just over three hours.

As he pulls onto the highway, he calls Cayden.

"You hit him on the back of his head?" Cayden asks.

"With a branding iron."

"We had a deal, Davis."

Napoleon can hear coughing through the phone.

"He's alive, isn't he?"

"Are you going to make me regret this?"

"No idea. When you're done with him, make your way up to the Eadwulf's Hampton property. Bring your friends."

"Your time's running out, you know? Another few hours and our contract's voided."

"I'll be there when the clock strikes midnight, my prince. Tiara and all."

"You wanna fill me in on the plan, here?"

"I would ... but you're ... breaking up ..."

"Davis?"

"Cough syrup ... asparagus ... scaffolding." He hangs up.

Two and a half hours later, he pulls up outside the gate of an enormous property protected by a guard box.

His timing is impeccable.

From where he's parked, he sees Adalyn stepping out of a tinted SUV and onto the gravel roundabout. She's followed by her father and a black woman he doesn't recognize, carrying a briefcase.

"You here for the funeral?" a security guard asks as he pulls up to the gate and rolls his window down.

"Yes, but I'm not on any list."

"Then I can't let you in," the guard says definitively.

"I understand, and I don't want to be an irritation. But would you mind doing me a favor and just radioing Ms. Eadwulf's liaison to let her know Napoleon Davis is here and the hitman she hired to kill her brother is in police custody."

"What?"

"Don't worry, she'll know what it means."

"Wait here," he says as he walks back into the guard box.

When he returns to the window a short while later, his overall demeanor has changed. "Pull up to the front and someone will meet you there."

"I appreciate it," he says, putting the sunglasses he'd found hanging from the driver's side visor back on.

As the front gate opens, he fills with dread at the thought that what he'd just done is probably going to be the easiest part of the next few hours.

"A pleasure to see you again, sir."

Wescott stands with his arms behind his back, watching Napoleon exit the car from on top a set of stone steps that lead up to the front door from the house's gravel driveway.

The whole property's vibe seems to be screaming, "Look at how many rocks I have!"

"Likewise, Wescott," he says as he approaches the base of the steps. "If only the circumstances weren't so gloomy."

"Yes, well, beggars can't be choosers," he smiles. "I seem to recall Ms. Eadwulf firing you if memory serves."

"She did, but I'm sure she'll want to hear what I have to say."

"I have no doubt of that."

As he reaches an equal playing field with Wescott, two more guards emerge from inside the open front door and move in unison to stand either side of him.

"Forgive me," Wescott says. "Before we can let you in, these two gentlemen need to pat you down."

"Understandable, this is a nice house. We wouldn't want it tainted with anything untoward."

"Our thoughts exactly."

The initial search is professional. But after confiscating nothing but his cellphone, their attitudes change.

"Why does it feel as if I'm on a boat all of sudden?"

One guard socks him in the stomach, and Napoleon keels over.

"Oh, dear. Stomachache?" Wescott asks.

Napoleon groans.

"I would ask that in the future, sir, you refrain from making any baseless accusations against my employer or any member of her house. Rest assured that any move they wish to make in opposition to you would be more than effective in alleviating the temptation. Their legal resources are . . . extensive."

"Limo driver, in-house counsel, *and* head of her security? I hope Adalyn pays you overtime."

"Not quite. Though I am duty-bound to serve Ms. Eadwulf in any capacity in which I am capable."

"Ah . . . and a late-night booty call."

Wescott frowns and nods to one of the guards, Napoleon's hit again. It takes a considerable amount of effort to keep himself from vomiting.

"Has anyone ever told you, you want for a filter?" Wescott asks.

"Heesh gon t' say shhh iret heem."

"What's that?"

The guards hoist Napoleon upright as he spits on the stone. "He's going to say she hired him."

"This hitman?"

"His story's elaborate, founded in half-truths. It'll be difficult to get it dismissed, even with *extensive legal resources*," he replies. "It wouldn't hurt your employer to know what he's going to say."

"And you know what his story will be, do you?"

"I do."

"How?"

"Because I'm a journalist."

Wescott chuckles as if the very idea is laughable. But when Napoleon doesn't join in, he stops.

"Let's say, hypothetically, I was to believe you," Wescott says. "What are you getting out of this?"

"He killed my friends."

"Ms. Eadwulf is aware of the *unfortunate* situation that arose at your residence as well as the incident at the club venue. We aren't, however, aware of any arrests having been made besides your own. How is it you came to be released might I ask?"

"They just let me go."

"Did they? Just like that?"

"Crazy, right?"

"And the hitman's arrest? It took place when?"

"I'd say a few hours ago."

"So we could expect a news release any minute now? Excellent! Why don't we wait and see? If you are telling the truth, it'll do wonders to corroborate your story."

"I got nothing else going on."

"I should think not."

Chapter 22

The foyer opens up into a common area with high ceilings and iron chandeliers that look older than Napoleon, Wescott, and the two security guards combined.

Staff members are still setting up for, based off the number of chairs, the small assembly of guests anticipated to attend.

The place has the feeling of an at-home cathedral. It's only reinforced by the priest going over his speech as he idles near the coffin and the enormous picture of Milo at the window's base.

"Right this way," Wescott says.

The guards nudge Napoleon forward, and the four of them head off down a marble corridor. As they approach a large oak door, Wescott gestures at a passing maid to open it.

She obliges. At which point, Napoleon finds himself in a large sitting room, the walls of which are lined with floor-to-ceiling bookshelves on three sides.

Two symmetrically placed spiral staircases on either side of the room lead up to a wooden walkway that protrudes out from the shelves about eight feet above their heads. The fourth wall is entirely comprised of a two-story window overlooking the gardens.

As he plunks down on one of the nearby couches, he looks out toward the hill at the other end of the garden to see several undertakers digging a grave.

I wonder how legal that is.

"Ms. Eadwulf is in a meeting at the moment and will see you when she's finished," Wescott says. "Can I get you anything while you wait?"

"You got any orange juice?" Napoleon asks.

Wescott gestures to the maid, who promptly exits.

"Security will be stationed outside the door. Don't be an idiot."

"K."

The second they've gone, he's on his feet. Adalyn knew he was here and, presumably, what he had told the guard at the front gate. Since it hadn't incentivized her to see him right away, he could assume whatever meeting she was in was more important to her.

A glance about the room reveals little in the way of options. He contemplates ramming the door with something, but common sense tells him that'd just attract the guard's attention. His deliberation is interrupted by a draft.

It's originating from an open window panel eleven feet off the ground. The walkway ends a good five feet to the right of that, so any chance of reaching it would be predicated on jumping over to it.

It's daunting and dangerous but doable.

Before mounting the stairs, he makes a pitstop at the bathroom and switches on the faucet; the maid needs to believe he's in there when she returns so that the guards aren't alerted.

Reaching the walkway, he takes a few seconds to map his route before moving to the other end of the railing to give himself space to build up speed.

Several quick breaths to steel himself later, and he's off.

As his foot connects with the banister, he propels himself off the walkway, through the air, and toward the open window. He only just manages to get his hands on the ledge as the momentum sends him swinging into the glass below.

While the window doesn't break, the force of contact does loosen the rigging keeping the window open, causing it to shut on his fingers, including his recently broken one.

Oh, you fuck! Fuck this fuckin' house with a toaster!

Realizing that the longer he hangs there, the more likely he is to fall, he quickly pushes the pain from his mind, props his feet up against the glass, and reopens the window.

He stumbles briefly as he almost misses the foothold he was aiming for on the other side. Luckily, he manages to prevent himself from falling at the last second.

"Great," he laughs to himself. "Now for the hard part."

Slowly, precariously, he starts moving across the walls of the house using various footholds and handholds. It's a hair-raising process that he quickly realizes is running the risk of going nowhere productive. All it would take is one of the many gardeners walking around the property to randomly look up and— "Hey! What are you doing up there?!"

"Oh, perfect," he mutters. "Nothing to see here, pal! Just a man realizing a lifelong dream of becoming a pigeon!"

"I'm calling security!"

"Please don't . . . Hello? Hel—shit."

He had planned to lower himself down onto the balcony of an open window several feet below. But now that he had the eye of some hourly workers who were, frankly, too dutiful for capitalism, he's incentivized to expedite his descent.

What was the saying again? Tuck and roll? Roll and tuck? That's not it. Unless it is. Dang.

He lets go of his handholds and screams as he drops onto the balcony. As he lands, he rolls forward through the window into the mansion, lands on his back, and knocks a vase off an inopportunely placed side table in the process.

"Eh gads!"

"What on Earth!"

"Napoleon?"

His answer comes as a groan as he sits up on his elbows and realizes he's in a schmancy-looking office.

Adalyn is sitting behind a large desk while Stanton and the woman are standing across from her. The woman's directing Stanton through a thick stack of paper that is resting on the desk.

"Well, what do you know?" He smiles. "That worked out."

"My God, man, do you realize what you've done?" Stanton asks. "That vase has more historical significance than most monuments!"

As he stands, Napoleon casts a fleeting look down at the vase's shattered ceramic remains. He kicks a piece with his shoe. "*Had*, I'm guessing."

"Insolent, uncultured—"

"Relax, old-timer, I'm about to make it up to you."

"Napoleon, I'm running the risk of losing my temper," Adalyn says. "So, I'd suggest you'd explain the meaning of this interruption as quickly as you can, before I—"

"Before you what?" He moves toward the desk. "Have me killed like you did Milo?"

"What?" Stanton asks, the vase forgotten.

"Haven't clued everybody into that little tidbit of information, have you? Adalyn here has been quite busy over these past couple of months. What with her hiring a hitman to take out her family, cofounding the development of a 'ground-breaking' new technology . . . orchestrating a coup."

Stanton takes a few steps back at mention of the last part.

"That's right, I know what you're doing here, sir," Napoleon says. "And while I'm no businessman, I do think before you sign over control of your company to your daughter, you should probably have all the information."

"What's he talking about?"

Adalyn's glaring at Napoleon now. And not in a nice way.

"Allow me to explain," he says. "Two days ago, I stumbled on Milo dying in an alley. I wasn't aware of it at the time, but he had managed to slip a flash drive into my pocket that contained a ton of information on a project he was working on called Plan Bee. Great name, by the way," he says sarcastically as he glances at Adalyn. "This project focused on developing artificial pollinators for the various plant species native to regions of land that use pesticides on their crops." He gestures to Stanton and Adalyn. "Regions where, as you two know, the *Bombus* are dying off at alarming rates, and the resulting lack of pollination is creating a ripple effect across the planet. This sort of invention would therefore be invaluable in restoring these regions. Not to mention the wonders it would do for the public image of the company producing them." He chuckles to himself. "Quite frankly, if that's all that it did, I wouldn't be here stopping you from relinquishing control, Stew."

Stanton does his best to seem taller than he is.

"But alas, this marvelous machine has itself a drawback, doesn't it, Adalyn?" Napoleon asks.

Adalyn's clenching the sides of her chair with a brutal vice grip.

"Anybody like to guess what that might be?"

The notary raises her hand. "Its manufacturing process is unsustainable?"

"No, it's—" Napoleon stops himself. "Actually, yeah . . . Wow, did you just guess that?"

"Ye—yeah?"

"Huh." He sticks out his bottom lip. "Well, anyway, surprise, surprise, this invention actually does more harm than good. Still, it's a multibillion-dollar idea. And there are always ways around the proverbial red tape of green interests, right? A handshake here, an envelope there, and all of a sudden, tomorrow's looking bee-autiful."

Surprisingly, no one laughs.

"But more importantly than all that other stuff combined"—he spins around to look at Adalyn—"it would provide Ms. Eadwulf here with the perfect opportunity to—"

"Establish her legacy," Stanton whispers.

Napoleon gestures as if to say "exactly" before adding, "If I learned anything from the introduction to psyche class I took in college. It's that those who have everything still want more." He shrugs. "But you are on track to inherit a company, right? It's a lot easier to enter a market under an existing wing than to grow a new bird."

"What?"

"Only, suddenly, you weren't. Because daddy dearest here decided he wanted to sell off the company for reasons I imagine have to do with the late wife passing?"

Stanton nods. "She was on a mission trip, helping to build homes for underprivileged families in—"

"Yeah, we don't need the whole backstory, but props for being willing to share." His focus shifts back to Adalyn. "So you paid to have your father discredited in the media and then accosted in front of all his peers with the hopes that it would be enough to convince him to step away from managing the company, putting you in the perfect position to facilitate its sale."

"Which she never intended on doing!" the notary exclaims.

"Correct!" Napoleon replies, pointing at her.

"How does this connect to my son?"

"There's a knife."

"A knife?"

"A knife. I didn't learn of it until fairly recently, but it appears to have been designed as a method of poisoning as much as to maim or cut. At first, I thought it was the hitman's, but the condition that he was in when I last saw him—"

"Wait, what?" Stanton asks.

Even Adalyn looks surprised by this.

"Story for another time," Napoleon says. "The condition he was in when I last saw him, the scar on his shoulder, and one detective's observation that it was an impressive piece of *engineering* suggest it was more likely used in an attack against him by someone else." He leans forward over the desk as he stares her down. "Someone who must have thought they would need an advantage in a fight. Someone who didn't want a paper trail giving away that they were armed. Someone who knew they were being watched."

Adalyn leans back in her chair, now seemingly calm.

"What part of the plan was Milo against?" Napoleon asks. "The coup? Or manufacturing the bees knowing what they'd do to the planet?"

"So this is what the hitman's going to claim, is it?"

"Is he wrong?" Stanton asks. "Is any of what's he said not to be believed?"

A brief pause hangs in the air.

"Yes."

Chapter 23

"What do you mean 'yes'?"

"Care to enlighten us?"

"Do I need to be here for this?" the notary asks.

"Was this the whole plan?" Adalyn asks. "You want the hitman to remain in jail, so you come here to ensure he can't leverage this story against us, knowing that we have the resources to denounce its credibility. But because you also think I'm responsible for hiring him, you wish to sabotage me?"

"Of course not," Napoleon says.

"No?"

"I also want the other five grand you owe me."

"Of course, you do."

"Five grand?" Stanton asks.

"She didn't tell you? Your daughter here hired me to snoop on you and the rest of the Eadwulf clan, claiming to suspect one of you of having hired the hitman. It's weird that didn't come up."

"Isn't it?" Adalyn smirks.

"You find all this amusing?" Stanton glares.

"Please, father," she sighs. "Whatever you think you know, I assure you, you're mistaken."

"But you did mastermind a plan to have him removed from his role as head of the company?" Napoleon raises an eyebrow.

"Well, yes, that's true."

"And you cultivated the development of Plan Bee with Milo as Chief Engineer?"

"I mean, he came to me with the initial design, but yes, that's more or less what happened."

"And when he discovered what the ecological fallout would be if you moved forward with manufacturing them, he wanted to shut it down. So you had him killed."

Adalyn leans back in her chair and interlocks her fingers.

"That's what happened, isn't it? You hired a professional killer to take out your own brother, and two of my friends got caught up in the crosshairs of your ambition."

"Sam," Adalyn says, addressing the notary trying to sneak out the door. "What time is it?"

Sam reads off the time.

"Good, then they're here already."

As she reaches for the intercom system on her desk, several security guards, including the two that were standing guard outside the door to Napoleon's waiting room, barge in and shout:

"Ms. Eadwulf! One of the gardeners has reported a prowler climbing the outside of the house and . . ." He trails off at the sight of Napoleon.

Napoleon waves at him.

"And it's taken you until now to get here?" Adalyn asks. "Did you get lost? Stop for a tank of gas?"

"Um, well—" the guard stutters nervously.

"Leave us," she continues. "And notify the authorities that my brother's killer can be found at our property in the Hamptons."

"I . . . Yes, ma'am, right away."

The guards leave disappointed.

"Right then." Adalyn stands up. "Shoes off, everyone. We don't want them to hear us coming on the marble."

She kicks off her heels and walks out. The rest of them briefly glance at one another with shared confusion before taking off their own shoes and following after her, if, for no other reason, than to make sure she's not running away.

"Adalyn," Stanton says, cutting through the silence of their walk. "Why are you leading us toward Milo's room?"

"Shhh, you'll spook them."

Faint moaning sounds are growing less faint as they near a door at the end of the hall.

"Them?" Napoleon asks.

Adalyn opens the door to reveal Kaleb and Polli entangled on the bed in the center of the room, playing what is no doubt a rousing game of hanky-panky, kinky-spanky.

Sam gasps.

"Holy shit." Napoleon laughs.

Polli screams as she vaults from the bed and darts for the bathroom, taking the bedsheets with her.

"What the hell!" Kaleb scrambles for a pillow to cover himself. "Knock much?"

"Lock the door while you're committing adultery much?"

"What have you done, boy?" Stanton asks, fuming.

"Oh my god!" Napoleon smacks his forehead. "Cocksucker!"

"Come again?"

"Yeah, the flash drive's passcode. Milo must've happened on a similar scene to the one in front of us. Only his had Polli in a . . . different position. Which explains why she wasn't at the bus stop with him!"

"Not to mention the bruises on his face," Adalyn adds.

"Bruises?"

"Kaleb was always the better fighter of the two of them. Have you noticed his hands?"

Stanton takes a step toward Kaleb. "You had your brother murdered because he caught you fucking his wife?!"

"Woah, murder?" Kaleb looks shocked. "What?"

"How long have you known?" Napoleon asks Adalyn.

"I've had a hunch ever since you mentioned the flash drive at the gala. Despite your otherwise impressive deduction, you overlooked one important detail. Plan Bee—I didn't pick the name, by the way—involved the three of us. We all stood to gain a lot from this enterprise."

"Until Milo found out about the affair and threatened to force Kaleb out," Napoleon says. "With your help, I'm assuming?"

Adalyn shrugs. "He called me late one night. Told me he had found out Kaleb and Polli were involved and asked if I knew anything about it. I'd already broached the subject with Kaleb and told him the situation needed rectifying for the sake of the business, presuming he'd interpret this to mean that he should come clean with Milo about what was going on." She wipes a tear from her eye. "Thinking this is what happened, I told him the truth. Next thing I knew, the company's servers had been wiped, and Milo was gone."

Everyone turns at the sound of something heavy being lifted off the ground to see Stanton storming toward Kaleb with a chair held over his head.

"Uh-oh," Sam says.

"Woah! Woah!!"

"Money?!" Stanton roars. "This was about money?!"

Bailing on his initial plan of standing there paralyzed, Kaleb jumps out of the bed with a pillow for pants, and darts to the furthest corner of the room as Napoleon tries to wrestle the chair away from Stanton.

"You stand to inherit billions!" he adds. "How much more money could you possibly need to justify fratricide, you good for nothing—"

"What the hell are you talking about, you fucking lunatic?!" Kaleb shouts back. "I didn't kill Milo!"

Silence.

"Really?" Sam asks.

"NO!"

"Prove it," Adalyn says.

Kaleb's eyes search the room for his pants. Finding them, he reaches into his wallet and retrieves a business card that he promptly tosses at Adalyn.

"After we fought, I went to a bar in Staten Island to cool off and ended up going home with one of the dancers." He points at the card Adalyn's now holding. "Call her, and she'll back me completely."

Stanton shakes Napoleon off of him. "That proves nothing."

"He's right," Adalyn says. "He was killed by a third party. You didn't need to be near him when he died, just a cellphone."

"Check my phone then!" Kaleb throws his arms up. "I haven't made any calls to any third party!"

"You could've used a burner."

"For fuck's sake!" Kaleb puts his pants back on. "I didn't kill my brother! So he threatened to kick me off the bee thing? How often did I actually show up to any board meetings?"

"Maybe you were jealous?" Adalyn proposes.

"Of what? He was a workaholic who spent fourteen hours a day in a science lab. I was already sleeping with his wife! He's not even better looking than me!"

"Well, if you didn't kill him," Stanton says, "then who exactly is responsible for my son's death?!"

"She is," Napoleon says.

They all turn to see that he's staring at the now open door to the bathroom. The room tenses. Standing there, with a cell phone and a bedsheet held around her frame in one hand, and a grenade in the other is Polli.

Chapter 24

"No sudden movements."

"Polli," Kaleb says, "what are you—"

"This grenade's live. Anybody tries anything funny, I drop it and we all get to see Milo a lot sooner than we anticipated."

"It was his wife all along?" Napoleon says out loud to no one in particular.

"Seem unoriginal," Sam adds, finishing his thought.

"Yet somehow," Adalyn says. "Not out of character."

"Blow it out your ass, you frigid shrew," Polli says. "You've no idea what my life's been like."

"Aw, poor Polli," Adalyn says mockingly. "Was two-timing my brother emotionally taxing for you? I understand. It must be hard marrying into the top 1 percent. To live with that constant reminder that you're of inferior stock. I know I couldn't handle it."

Damn.

"Ouch," Sam says.

"I mean, really," Stanton adds.

"Way to go for the jugular," Kaleb smiles.

"I'm confused," Polli says. "Do you all want to die?"

The room goes quiet.

"Who's got their phone?" She gestures to Adalyn, Stanton, and Kaleb. "Out of the three of you."

The room stays quiet.

"Fine, you wanna play it that way?" She releases the sheet to free up a hand so she can dial a number. "That's how we'll play it."

The room reacts simultaneously.

"Oi!"

"Really?"

"For goodness' sake!"

"Really wish I wasn't hard right now."

"You might want to get that mole looked at."

She finishes dialing. Seconds later, Adalyn's phone starts ringing.

"Oh good," Polli says. "I need you to log into the company's checking account and wire a $100 million to the account number I've just texted you."

"Wowzers."

"You do, do you?"

"A hundred million?"

"You've lost your mind!"

"How do you not have pores?"

"The company's worth a hundred times that." She studies her cuticles. "You'll hardly miss it. Think of it as a generous endowment to an up-and-comer. Because I have a brilliant business venture of my own that could use some startup seeding."

"Oh yeah? What?" Adalyn asks. "A production company that finances star vehicles for you to launch your acting career?"

Several seconds pass before Polli responds. "Maybe."

"Typical."

"Come on, really?"

"A production company?!"

"That's a tough business to break into."

"Can I please leave?" Sam asks again, gesturing to the door. "I don't feel like I'm a part of this and—"

"Nobody's going anywhere!" Polli shouts. "Why am I not receiving a notification, Adalyn?"

"It's. Pending." She says through gritted teeth.

"You're actually giving it to her?" Stanton asks.

"She's holding a grenade!"

TING! Polli looks at her phone. "Good, it went through. Now all we need to do is . . ." Her voice trails off at the sound of police sirens getting louder. A glance out of the closest window confirms her fears.

"No," she whispers. "No, no, no, who called the police?!"

Napoleon, Sam, and even Stanton, subtly point at Adalyn.

"Wha—" Adalyn remarks. "Dad?!"

"Don't 'dad me. Half an hour ago, you were preparing to force me out."

"Excuse me for thinking you needed a vacation."

"Enough!" Polli shouts. "Whose car is that out front?!"

It's Adalyn's turn to point. Following her lead, the rest of the room does the same, except for Napoleon, who, reluctantly, raises his hand.

"Then you're my hostage. Here's the plan. You and I are going to calmly walk down to the driveway and out the gate past the police."

"Oh." Napoleon sucks in a mouthful of air between his teeth. "Yeah, don't know how successful of a plan that's likely to be. The police aren't exactly known for, you know . . . not shooting people who look like me on sight. Especially if we're standing next to naked white ladies. How about this though?" He holds up the car keys. "I've got the keys here." He points to Stanton. "And there's a Captain of industry right there. Why not have him drive you out of here?"

Stanton raises an eyebrow.

"Makes more sense if you ask me," Napoleon adds. "He's a member of the Fortune 500, he carries a lot of influence in big social circles, he's white, so, you know, points for that. Police are *way* less likely to shoot him than they are me."

"Ah, but you're forgetting," says Stanton, "that I have been nothing but chastised and berated in the media recently. And after my recent outburst at the gala, support from those in my social sphere is bound to be rather low." He turns to Polli. "You would be much better off using Adalyn here."

"Yikes."

"Unbelievable," Adalyn says.

Stanton continues, "She's a well-respected, accomplished, businesswoman. A shining example of tomorrow's America. And it would be a PR nightmare for law enforcement if she was placed in harm's way."

"Hang on a second," Adalyn interjects. "What about Kaleb? I mean he's . . . he's . . . I've got nothing."

Kaleb raises his fists in triumph. "Ha-ha!"

"Well, now everyone's coming," Polli says, throwing on a kimono. "Let's go, single file out the door, anyone runs, and we all go up in smoke."

As they file out the room and down the corridor, Wescott and the maid from earlier emerge from a side door. Hair frizzy, uniforms creased, it's clear to Napoleon that whatever tasks the two had been assigned that day, what they'd just finished doing probably wasn't on the list.

"Wescott, thank God!"

"Ma'am?"

"Back inside!" Polli shouts as she waves the grenade in their faces. "Don't come out until you've got wrinkles!"

The maid obliges right away. Wescott debates it for half a second longer, his eyes lingering on Adalyn. Then he too obliges.

"You really think you'll get away with this?" Stanton asks.

"Kind of."

"Where'd you even get a grenade?" Napoleon asks.

"Please," she says. "I'm in show business."

"Hang on," Adalyn says a little while later as they're walking down the stairs to the foyer. "How'd you get it past security, everyone was vetted before being allowed in the house?"

"Fanny packing," she says matter-of-factly.

"Fanny packing?" Sam asks, trying to keep it together.

"It's when you carry stuff around in your vagina." Kaleb grins. "Takes pussy to die for to a whole new level, am I right?"

"Ugh!"

"What?"

"You're disgusting."

"There's something wrong with your head, boy."

"Oh, I'm the freak? She's carrying weapons-grade explosives in her babymaker!"

Sam breaks down.

Outside on the driveway, Cayden and Douglas exit their patrol car. Cayden frowns at the sight of the four Hampton beat cops who'd come as backup. Their turf meant they'd more than likely be unaccustomed to a 10-10Y and were liable to develop itchy trigger fingers should things escalate.

"Fuck, that was a long drive." Douglas cups his lower back. "Remind me what we're doing here again?"

"Dispatch got a call saying that whoever killed Milo Eadwulf was at this address," Cayden says. "Seeing as we have the hitman in custody, I assume that means Napoleon must've actually figured out who it was that hired him."

"Yeah, yeah, yeah, but what are *we* doing here? This isn't our jurisdiction. Anything we find is just gonna have to be turned over to the Hampton hand jobs over there."

"I think you're just bitter because my plan worked."

"Did you not hear the lieutenant's voicemail?" Douglas asks. "The feds are *pissed!* The only reason we haven't been fired yet is because we haven't done our paperwork!"

"When we bring in the contractor—"

"What if it is Davis?" Douglas asks.

"I'm not having this conversation again."

"How'd he know the killer would show up to his place? What if this is all just part of his plan to get away with having hired the guy?"

"Then I'll apologize."

"If I've had to sit in the car for three hours just to pick him up again, I'm going to kick you in the dick."

"Attention law enforcement!"

Both detectives and all four cops turn to see the Eadwulfs and associates emerging from the mansion. Training takes over at the sight of the half-dressed woman holding a hand grenade, and their guns are drawn as they dart for cover behind their cruisers.

All six sights are now aimed at Polli.

"Kindly lay down your weapons!" she shouts. "Then move the vehicles out from in front of the gate and throw your keys into that shrubbery over there!"

"Drop your weapon!" Douglas shouts back.

"Do you not understand how a grenade works?"

"Let's everybody just remain calm," Cayden says, picking up where Douglas is falling short. "I'm sure we can figure something out here."

"The situation isn't open to negotiation. Stanton, Adalyn, Napoleon, and myself will be leaving here in that car with Napoleon as our driver."

"All right," Kaleb whispers to Sam. "We don't have to go."

He tries to get her to fist bump, but she just stares at him.

"And you will do nothing to interfere!" Polli says. "Or I'll release my hand, and everyone here will go bang!"

Everyone pauses for a moment at her phrasing.

"Not like that!"

"Let's talk about this," Cayden says.

"You have to the count of three . . . One!"

"I've got a clear shot," Douglas whispers to Cayden. "There's a delay after the spoon is released. If we tell them to run as I shoot, they may be able to make it far enough away before it explodes."

"That's a big maybe!"

"Two!"

"Well, what do you think we should do?"

"Two and a half!"

She never says three.

Stanton chooses to capitalize on her focus being held elsewhere. For as much as he missed Lillian, he had no interest in expediting their reunion.

Her death, though tragic, had also been poetically ironic.

To think a pesticide heiress would fall victim to food riddled by the very chemicals her company manufactured. She was old, and it hadn't taken much to shake her constitution.

As Polli is counting, he slowly moves behind her, his center of gravity low enough that sending her careening over the concrete steps will require little of him.

Without so much as a second thought for the hostages, he races back into the house to put as much distance between himself and the explosion as possible.

His staff, unaccustomed to seeing him run and already shaken and confused by the commotion outside, do nothing as he continues past them toward the indoor pool.

As he enters the pool room, he takes a deep intake of air before throwing himself into the water with no intention of resurfacing until he's heard a muffled pop.

Most of those who remain, cops and hostages alike, stand in paralyzed anticipation as the grenade flies out of Polli's hand and lands on the gravel driveway.

Most of them.

Cayden coughs as an odd clarity slowly washes over him. He rushes forward. It's a feeling he's experienced only one other time. The intensity of it hasn't diminished with repetition, and yet he feels better about the implications this time around. There's a nobility to dying in the line of duty that cancer can't quite match.

So it upsets him that much more when Napoleon manages to throw himself on top of the grenade first.

Chapter 25

"Why would you do that?"

"You're giving me shit?" Napoleon pulls the oxygenator away from his mouth. "You were gonna do the same thing."

He's sitting on the back bumper of an ambulance, wrapped in a blanket. The EMT tending to him had insisted on both it and the oxygenator. Despite his efforts to assure her it wouldn't be necessary, she'd had none of it.

"It's my job to protect and serve." Cayden's standing with his arms crossed. "Not yours."

"Can't you just thank me for saving your life and move on?"

"You saved shit. The grenade was a fake."

"Surely it's the thought that counts though."

"How did you know?"

"I didn't." Napoleon wraps the blanket around himself tighter. "Just a hunch. More of a stereotype really. I figured actors typically have big egos. They must do, right? To want to be in front of a camera all day? Would that kind of hubris really let Polli put herself in harm's way like that? She was probably going to drop the whole farce the moment we were in the clear."

Cayden's eyes widen as Napoleon brings the oxygenator back up to his mouth. "How's that for a high-stakes acting exercise?"

"You gambled with your life, and that was your hunch?"

Napoleon responds by pulling what looks to Cayden like a button off his shirt and tossing it to him.

"What's this?" Cayden asks.

"That right there is how the hitman figured out James had the flash drive, and I didn't. He used it to bug our apartment, and he overhead James offering to take the drive to spread the risk of death between us. I turned it on the moment I pulled up to the Tribune."

"Tribune?"

"I'll send you the address. I have a feeling you're going to want to speak to a woman named Cindy Li. That is if she hasn't left town. It has her confession on it, as well as several other eye-opening testimonials. And since I'm not a cop, and it's not police-issued gear, you can file it away as anonymous evidence without having to worry a judge will throw it out as unauthorized surveillance footage."

Cayden has to fight the urge to let his jaw drop open.

"It's transmitting to a monitor in that car by the way." Napoleon gestures to the hatchback before tossing Cayden the key. "You should probably take it in as evidence."

Cayden briefly looks at the key in his hand and then back at Napoleon. "Not a vigilante, huh?"

Douglas, who's been loitering nearby, acting as though he wasn't eavesdropping, takes this opportunity to approach the two of them.

"Look." He clears his throat as he turns toward Napoleon. "I just wanted to say . . ." His voice trails off as he fails to find the words. After several seconds of tense silence, he then does the unexpected and extends his hand out toward Napoleon. "A deal's a deal."

Napoleon's surprised but makes no move to offer his own. Douglas realizes, quickly withdraws his own, and nods as though he understands.

"We're going to take off now," Cayden says. "You want a ride back to the city?"

"I'll take a cab."

Cayden nods before tossing Douglas the car key. Without another word, he turns and heads back toward his patrol car. Douglas lingers half a second longer before turning and walking off in the direction of the hatchback.

While the three of them were talking, uniform officers were taking statements, corralling reporters, and escorting all the complicit parties into cruisers to be taken in for processing.

True to form, Polli hadn't gone without making a scene. As it slowly dawned on everyone that the grenade wasn't going to explode, she made a break for it across the grass. Some of the officers had pointed guns, demanding she'd stop.

When she didn't, they chased after her instead.

Napoleon, among others, had stood and smiled at the sight of her bobbing and weaving in and out of their grasp as she attempted to reach the perimeter of the property. In the end, it took four officers to subdue and cuff her.

Adalyn's arrest caused the least amount of fuss. She raised no objections and made no effort to run. Napoleon doubted she'd even spend the night in jail.

Kaleb, equally as confident as his sister, though not quite as poised, couldn't seem to help himself and decided to pass the time trying to make his arresting officers laugh.

Stanton Eadwulf's body was found floating in the pool. An initial examination revealed water in his lungs and a blood clot in his heart. The cause of death had been easy to deduce.

The excitement of the day, his years of alcohol abuse, and his brief stint of physical exertion had simply made his heart pop. Given that he'd been in the pool at the time, it resulted in an involuntary intake of water that thrust him into unconsciousness.

Funny, Napoleon thinks. *In his want to live, he killed himself.*

Napoleon's currently watching the emergency responders file out the front gate; off to wherever duty was calling next.

Five minutes later, he's shooed off the back bumper by his attending EMT, who having assessed his vitals, decides that he's fine and there's no longer any reason for her and her colleague to hang around.

The idea of asking them for a ride passes through his head briefly but is quickly dismissed. With a friendly wave, the ambulance pulls out onto the road and disappears.

Suddenly, he is alone.

That is until the hairs on the back of his neck stand up, and he turns to see the funeral priest loitering atop the stone steps. Despite the recent events, he seems thoroughly at ease.

"I've told the authorities I'm not leaving till the man lying in the coffin in there is sent into the next life with God's grace," he says as if it were the most normal sentence in the world.

"Uh-huh."

"It seems his family will be unable to attend the service."

"He's probably better off."

"Perhaps." The priest chuckles as he descends the stones to stand eye-level with Napoleon. "But wouldn't you want people at your funeral?"

Napoleon casts a glance back at the front gate, and the priest leaves him to his thoughts. But quickly realizing how much of a shit show wallowing in those is likely to be, Napoleon heads inside shortly thereafter.

The priest's already standing at the head of the room when he enters, delivering his sermon to the others who've also been guilted into attendance.

A lot of what the priest is saying connects with Napoleon's personal understanding of who Milo had been. A lot doesn't. His funeral portrait shows the face of a man in much better condition than the one Napoleon had found in the alley.

Less blood and anguish, more hair gel.

Napoleon's eyes then migrate to the table of refreshments in the corner of the room. The food tempts him but not like the hundred-year-old bottle of wine sitting among its less impressive friends.

He picks it up as he approaches; it's open but not empty. He carries it over, sans glass, to an empty seat in the row of chairs set up to face the head of the room.

He's about to sit down when the priest says, "We will now follow the coffin bearers up to what will be Milo's final resting place."

A clock radio resting on a nearby shelf catches Napoleon's eye as he follows the procession over to a side door that leads out into the yard. A wireless clock radio.

He fumbles with the dial until he's able to find a song that somewhat passes for appropriate.

I've been in love, and I've been to war,
I've been fun, and I've been a bore,
Been rolling in cash and a next level of poor,

You best believe I've been here before,

The coffin bearers are the first to leave the hill after the body is lowered into the grave, followed not long after by Rose, Wescott, and other staff, including the priest.

I've been committed, and I've been a whore,
Top of the world with my back to the floor,
Made some mistakes I can't seem to ignore,
You best believe I've been here before,

Before Sam leaves, she asks Napoleon if he wants to walk down with her. He tells her he'll catch up.

A glance down at the bottom of the hill reveals the undertakers are on the way up with shovels.

Cause I've been married, and I've been divorced,
I've been brave as well as shook to my core,
Tongue-tied despite having built a rapport,
You'd know I'm a lion if you'd heard me—

The song cuts out as the clock radio dies.

He stands there for several minutes after that, admiring the view of the Atlantic from beneath the changing leaves of a large oak tree. The faint smell of campfire is dancing in the warm breeze. And there's a cloud . . . shaped like Polli's boobs.

A bee lands on his shoulder.

The immoderateness of the symbolism prompts him to look up at the sky briefly before he heads off down the hill, drinking the wine bottle as he goes. He had been wearing the tux for nearly twenty-four hours, and it needed dry cleaning.

About the Author

Joe Harrison is an actor, filmmaker, and award-winning screen-writer. The Unpaid Internship is his debut novel.

Printed in Great Britain
by Amazon